THE GATE AT THE GREY WOLF STAR

Perseus Gate – Episode 1

By M. D. Cooper

Cover Art by Andrew Dobell
Editing by Tee Ayer

FOREWORD

It has been ten years since I wrote my first short story about Jessica, a scrappy Terran Bureau of Investigations agent who found herself wrapped up in some pretty incredible events.

She's always managed to make a name for herself, from an unwilling stowaway on the *Intrepid* to becoming one of Tanis's closest friends, Jessica is a key player in the greater Aeon 14 story.

I did my best to write this tale so that you can pick it up without needing to read the other tales that come before it, and the short synopsis below should give you enough context to do so.

However, if you first want to read what came before, you can start all the way at the beginning with Outsystem, or you can begin at the mid-point and read Destiny Lost, followed by New Canaan before you dive into The Gate at the Grey Wolf Star.

No matter where you pick up the story, I am certain you're going to love this tale. Its full of mystery, some fun hijinks, and a climax unlike any you've seen in any other Aeon 14 story.

M. D. Cooper

TABLE OF CONTENTS

SABRINA'S MISSION

Sera Tomlinson knew that her father, President of the Transcend Interstellar Alliance, would not treat well with the New Canaan colonists.

He would allow them to settle in, and get comfortable on their new worlds; then force their hand, by demanding that they turn over their advanced technology to further build up the Transcend's military. Or else.

To counter her father, Sera sent *Sabrina* and her former crew into the Inner Stars to find Finaeus, her exiled uncle.

No one had expected it to be easy, but after nine long years, Jessica, Cargo and the rest of the crew tracked Finaeus down in the Ikoden System.

Finaeus agreed to travel with the crew of *Sabrina* to New Canaan, but they were attacked by unknown agents. Fearing the difficulties the four-year journey to New Canaan would present, Finaeus convinced the crew to travel to a secret Transcend base, deep within the Inner Stars.

There the Transcend operates a Jump Gate, massive Ford-Svaiter mirror that will facilitate a near-instantaneous voyage to New Canaan.

Or so they hope.

SABRINA'S CREW

Cargo – Ship's Captain
Cheeky – Pilot
Erin – AI embedded in Nance
Finaeus – Passenger
Jessica – First Mate
Hank – AI embedded in Cargo
Iris – AI embedded in Jessica
Nance – Bio/Engineer
Piya – AI embedded in Cheeky
Sabrina – Ship's AI
Trevor – Supercargo and muscle

NOTE: When *Sabrina* is italicized, it refers to the ship, but if Sabrina is not italicized, it refers to the AI. Yes, this would be much simpler if the ship and AI did not share the same name, but you try telling that to Sabrina!

Just so you stay on her good side, never call the ship "**the** *Sabrina*", it really gets on her last synthetic neuron.

PROLOGUE: CARETAKER

STELLAR DATE: 04.17.8938 (Adjusted Years)
LOCATION: *Sabrina* docked at Kruger Station
REGION: Ikoden System, Mika Alliance Space

Meet me.

The voice crept into Nance's mind once more. She knew it wasn't over the Link; she had disconnected herself from the shipnet, fearful of the words she continued to hear over and over again.

She should be alone in her own head.

Meet me, the voice insisted again, pushing at the bounds of her consciousness as though it were trying to trigger something beneath.

Nance forced it away, made herself think about her work, about the faulty backup fuel regulator that needed fixing. She thought about the part number, the supplier, where she would place it while she removed the existing regulator, the color of the box. Anything but the voice.

Meet me.

It was louder now, and Nance knew the voice was *wrong*, but she didn't know what to do. Who should she talk to? Her AI, Erin, was new to her, and might think she was crazy—surely if Nance *was* crazy, an AI from the *Intrepid* would notice. Wouldn't she?

The thought crossed Nance's mind that maybe Erin was the one doing this to her.

Meet me now.

No, it didn't feel like Erin, it didn't feel like anyone else—it felt like herself.

Where? she finally replied.

Onstation. I'll guide you.

It's third shift, Nance thought to herself—and whatever else she was talking to. *Someone will notice if I leave.*

Meet me.

It was clear that the voice could not be rationalized with. She would have to venture onto the station to find out what was going on.

What about Erin? Won't she wonder where I'm going?

Erin is asleep. She won't know about this, the voice replied in her mind.

Asleep? Nance asked. She didn't even know that AI *could* sleep.

Meet me.

Nance rose from her bed and glanced around the room at her collection of dolls ringing the room on their shelves. Her gaze shifted to the row of hazmat suits hanging neatly in their racks. She resisted the urge to don one, before walking to her closet.

Within hung several shipsuits, pants, shirts and jackets—plus a few dresses that Cheeky had purchased for her, though Nance didn't think those fit the occasion.

She pulled on a pair of dark blue pants, a tight tank-top shirt, and a soft jacket. It looked just right for wandering around the station late in its night cycle and not attracting any specific attention. She pulled her hair on top of her head and twisted it in a tight bun before slipping her feet into a pair of low boots.

A laugh and a pair of footfalls echoed down the corridor and she froze. Jessica and Trevor were still up—engaged in their usual shenanigans, no doubt. Then, she heard Jessica's cabin door close and she released the breath she had been holding.

Meet me.

The voice sounded the same, but somehow still managed to seem more insistent. Maybe it was the repetition that was making her think that.

Nance palmed her door open and peered into the hall. It was empty.

She crept down its length to the ladder that lead to the ship's cargo deck. Her boots sounded loud to her ears, but she knew that a set of soft footfalls in the crew corridor would not raise any questions—even late at night.

Once down the ladder and on the ship's cargo deck, she picked up the pace, moving toward the smaller aft port hatch. She was reaching for the controls to open it when Sabrina spoke into her mind.

<Hey, Nance, what's up?>

She hadn't re-enabled her Link access…had the voice? Frozen, Nance tried to think of what to say, but no plausible lie coming to mind.

You just need a walk, can't sleep, clearing your head, the voice suggested.

<Hey Sabrina, I just need to clear my head and take a walk—was having trouble sleeping.>

<OK,> Sabrina replied. *<Senzee should be safe—not like we're on Chittering Hawk anymore—but be careful. Call if you need help. I'll send the cavalry.>*

Nance gave a mental smile in response. *<I'm sure I'll be OK.>*

<OK, have fun on your walk.>

The airlock's outer door slid open, and Nance stepped out onto the station's J12 cargo dock.

Few people were present, though she could see at least a dozen or so before the dock curved away to the left and the right. The lights were dim, everything cast in the green and red glow from the indicators hovering over the docking portals, showing where ships were docked, and which berths were empty.

She was just wondering which way to go when the voice in her head said, *Left*.

For the next thirty minutes, Nance followed the voice's directions, moving deeper into Senzee Station, beyond the commercial districts surrounding the docks, through several residential areas, and finally to an area filled with low-rent housing.

Despite Sabrina's assurances of relative safety, Nance was starting to wish that she had brought a weapon. Then the voice spoke again. *In here.*

The portal it directed her toward lay open, looming ominously with only darkness beyond. It looked exactly like the sort of place she had no desire to enter. She tried to turn back, but her legs wouldn't move.

"What?" she whispered hoarsely.

Enter.

Nance couldn't believe this was happening. It was like a nightmare—stars, she hoped it was a nightmare. For a full minute she wrestled with her body, trying to move it away from the dark entrance, only to find that she could move forward, but not back.

<Erin! Erin, help! Please Erin, wake up. Help!> Nance screamed inside her mind, but her AI didn't respond; it was almost as though Erin wasn't there. She tried to raise the ship instead. *<Sabrina, I'm in trouble. Send the cavalry, Sabrina!>*

Then, her right leg took a step forward on its own, followed by her left. She began to scream as her body refused to obey her commands and carried her over the threshold toward a strange, glowing figure which appeared out of thin air.

Welcome back, Myrrdan.

Nance tried to speak, to ask the figure what it wanted, but no words came out. She was just a passenger in her own body.

"Surely you know that this is not me, this is just a shadow, an impression I placed within this woman." Nance heard the words come from her mouth—something else was in control now.

"Of course I do," the glowing figure said.

Nance watched it approach her, feeling as though she should be trembling with fear, but her body stood rock still. She found herself becoming detached from the situation, and wondered how the figure had materialized. It didn't look like a holoprojection; it seemed to be solid, yet it also appeared to be made of light.

Its form was vaguely humanoid, but taller and thinner. Its hands reached almost to its knees and it lifted them to her face to stroke her cheek.

"I had wondered if I would ever see you again—if Tanis Richards had found you out."

Nance a ripple of laughter in her throat. "She thinks she has. I staged a little death scene with Jessica. It cost me one of my favorite shells, but it was worth it."

"The TBI agent," the figure said. "That was a risk…bringing her aboard."

Nance realized she knew this story. Tanis had related it to them one night, when she'd told them the true story of the Battle for Victoria. How a fiend from Sol had taken the form of one of their crew, and killed Jessica's wife—though Tanis had said that Myrrdan did not survive the engagement.

Apparently Tanis could be wrong.

Am I Myrrdan now? Nance thought to herself.

No. The voice replied.

"I've done what you asked," Nance's voice said aloud. "I made sure that the *Intrepid* came to Kapteyn's star, and I made sure they used their picotech."

"*I* set that in motion," the figure said.

"Well, yes, from your end in Sirius," Nance's voice said. "By the way, I never learned your name when last we met."

"That is correct," the figure replied. "I go by many names, but you may call me The Caretaker."

"OK, Caretaker." Nance's possessor nodded. "I got the *Intrepid* here, in the future, and they used their picotech—which is what I suspect you wanted."

"It is." The Caretaker inclined its head in agreement. "Though the ship's disappearance into the dark layer afterward was unexpected. Sera Tomlinson is to credit for that, from what the evidence shows."

"Yes," the Myrrdan shadow replied. "That is her name. She has also set up a rendezvous with the *Intrepid* and the Transcend's diplomats soon to secure a colony world."

The glowing figure inclined its head, as though it were deep in thought, or perhaps communicating with someone else.

"That can work," it said finally. "It's all too soon—they came out of the streamer five-hundred-years before we'd intended."

"What do you need me to do now?" the Myrrdan shadow asked.

The figure lifted its head and looked up. Nance could almost make out a smile on its strange features.

"You? We have no more use for you. You're one of our most distasteful tools—effective, but distasteful. We will expunge you from this woman—though we will use her for our purposes now. She will eventually return to the *Intrepid* where we will clean up the loose end that you represent.

STELLAR APPROACH

STELLAR DATE: 07.22.8938 (Adjusted Years)
LOCATION: *Sabrina*, Near Gisha Station
REGION: DSM Ring, Grey Wolf System

Jessica stood in the center of *Sabrina*'s bridge, arms akimbo as she stared at the forward holodisplay of the Grey Wolf Star wrapped in its massive mining ring.

The thing still boggled her mind. Sure, several Terran mining operations back in Sol had begun starlifting mass off Sol before the *Intrepid* had left—something that had upset the ecoterrorists to no end—but this was an entirely different matter.

"Still quite the sight, isn't it?" Finaeus asked as he approached Jessica.

She turned her head and threw the ancient terraformer a glance. The man was stealthy for being millennia old. She hadn't heard him enter the bridge—and her ears were far above standard fare.

<He's probably using his nanocloud to mask his sounds,> Iris, the AI with whom Jessica shared her mind, said.

<On the ship? Seems excessive,> Jessica said.

<He's been in exile—on the run, most likely—for a very long time. I bet paranoia is his modus operandi now.>

"I've been staring at that damn thing for nine days now, and I still can't believe that it exists," Jessica replied audibly to Finaeus.

"You should see Airtha some day," Finaeus said, a wistful tone in his voice. "The star is bigger than the Grey Wolf, we pulled a lot of mass off it—making it oh…about Saturn-sized. But we made good use of all that carbon when we made the ring."

"Oh yeah?" Cheeky asked from the pilot's seat.

Jessica had almost forgotten that Cheeky was down there; neither of the two women had spoken in the hour before Finaeus arrived and broke the silence.

"Yeah," Finaeus chuckled. "We built a ring out of carbon, massive, makes the old stuff in Sol look like kid's toys. Way out—much further than Saturn's outer rings were from Saturn itself. Just a gleaming diamond ring around the star. Threw a few terrestrial worlds in orbit too...high inclination so they only get short eclipses from the ring. It was my greatest work...."

"Was?" Jessica asked.

"Oh, well, it's still there, but my core-damned brother gave it to *her*—now I don't think of it as much as *my* work as *her* den."

"Who?" Jessica asked.

Finaeus pulled a tired smile across his face. "Another time, perhaps, dear."

Jessica frowned. Finaeus certainly liked his enigmas. She hoped that he would be of use to Sera. What was this man capable of—especially after being exiled—that could grant Sera whatever leverage she thought she needed?

Cheeky snorted. "Well, this star mining operation may be magnificent, but it's a nightmare to fly into. Those black holes they're spinning around the star create killer EM and gravitational fields."

"And just think," Finaeus said. "Krissy is taking us in the easy way. Even with graviton field dampeners, your ship would be ripped to shreds from the shearing forces on other approaches."

"Yeah, I can see that shit on scan. Not even sure our stasis shields could deal with that. Gravity can still reach through them—we'd probably have to go solid bubble."

"Solid bubble falling toward a star," Jessica said. "Not my idea of a good time."

"There must be a doldrums ahead, otherwise they wouldn't have a station that far in," Cheeky said. "Any idea how long 'til we hit it?"

Finaeus shrugged. "Your guess is as good as mine. They've added more black holes…upped the rotation since I last looked it over. Can't be too much further though. We can see Gisha Station and it's not that big."

"Not big?" Cheeky asked. "Thing's at least a hundred-and-fifty-kilometers in diameter."

"Yeah, but it's next to a ring wrapped around a star." Jessica frowned. "Just about anything looks small next to that."

"Good point," Cheeky replied.

<Got comm,> Sabrina said. *<Just docking instructions. A berth in an interior bay down on the station's hub.>*

"Great. Interior berth." Cheeky shook her head as she rose and stretched. "Jess, do a girl a favor and take the helm for a bit? I want to get dressed and eat before taking her in."

"Sure," Jessica replied as she took in an appreciative look at Cheeky's ass. "Find something that covers more than just a few square centimeters, will you? Sera says these Transcend types are prudes."

Cheeky paused at the bridge's entrance and looked back at Jessica with a raised eyebrow. "*I* can cover up no problem. What are *you* going to do, doll-girl?"

"I can dress down." Jessica shrugged.

Finaeus snorted. "I've been on this ship for weeks and I find both your statements dubious at best. Not that I'm complaining. It's not often I'm in the company of such fine women."

Cheeky laughed and left the bridge, while Jessica slipped into the pilot's seat. She initiated a flight-control systems analysis and glanced down at herself.

In the Inner Stars, her lavender skin and hair barely drew a moment's notice. Even her exaggerated proportions were not extreme compared with many of the men and women she had seen.

Still, all her clothing was tight, revealing, or both—usually both. Could the Transcend really be so uptight that these simple physical tweaks were frowned upon?

"Was Sera pulling our leg about how uptight things are in the Transcend?" Jessica asked Finaeus.

"Transcend is a big place," he said with a shrug. "There are places where people have completely done away with physical bodies, places where they've turned themselves into weird dolphin things and live in oceans. But at Airtha, and where the military is concerned? Yeah, I'd say she's not far off."

"Don't tell Cheeky about the places with the dolphin-people. She's going to want to see how they are between the sheets…or the kelp…whatever."

Finaeus laughed. "I'll keep it to myself, but I suspect that there is little in this galaxy that Cheeky has not sampled."

Jessica shook her head. On that subject she was in complete agreement with Finaeus.

USURPED

STELLAR DATE: 07.22.8938 (Adjusted Years)
LOCATION: TSS *Regent Mary*, Near Gisha Station
REGION: DSM Ring, Grey Wolf System

Admiral Krissy slipped the final button into its hole at her collar and tugged on her uniform's jacket to ensure it was straight. She adjusted one of her ribbons and nodded. That would do nicely.

Finaeus…Finaeus was a handful on the best of days. She wanted him to remember how things stood, and who was in charge when they met.

<Message from Gisha,> Hemdar, the *Regent Mary*'s ship-AI informed Admiral Krissy. *<It's from Stationmaster Lloyd.>*

Krissy frowned, wondering what reason Lloyd would have to reach out to her personally. Perhaps it was to request a change of docking location for the *Sabrina*. He probably wouldn't like that she had given the starfreighter an interior hub berth.

Keep your enemies close, and all that.

<Thank you, Hemdar,> Krissy replied and accepted the connection. *<Stationmaster, I trust all is well on Gisha?>*

<Not as well as normal,> Lloyd replied with a mental grimace.

Krissy wasn't surprised he would say that. Lloyd preferred things to stay the same—exactly the same—forever. Even her coming in early—with or without a foreign ship—would have upset him.

<Is this about the docking assignment,> Krissy asked.

Lloyd shook his head in her mind. *<No, but I'm not happy about that either. This news is much less pleasant than a potential antimatter explosion from some Inner Stars garbage scow. I have a Grey Division ship on final approach.>*

"Shit," Krissy swore aloud. Grey Division was the last thing she wanted to deal with right now. <*ETA?*> she asked Lloyd.

<*Before you. An hour at least.*>

<*Thanks, Lloyd. I owe you one,*> Krissy replied.

<*Count's a lot higher than that, Admiral,*> Lloyd said as he closed the connection.

"Civilians," Krissy said with a sigh as she leaned against her cabin's bulkhead and closed her eyes for a moment.

Although, she'd take civilians any day over dealing with Grey Division.

No one—at least no one that *she* knew—had a clue exactly who Grey Division reported to. Their official title was the 137th Division of Space Force Strategic Research, but few believed that their core mandate was research.

The consensus was that they were the military version of The Hand, without the pretense at diplomacy.

<*Think it'll be anyone we know?*> Krissy asked Hemdar.

<*You know seven Greys, and I know nine, there are three we've met together. None of them are in the least pleasant to be around. Do you prefer one of those, or shall we hope it's someone new who isn't absolutely horrible?*>

<*Well, I always prefer the devil I know,*> Krissy replied. <*But maybe in this case we can hope for a new Grey that's not a devil at all.*>

Hemdar gave the mental equivalent of a snort. <*Sure, keep dreaming.*>

Krissy pushed herself off the wall, gave her uniform a final tug, and palmed her cabin's door open.

Outside, a pair of lieutenants, followed by a commander, rushed down the hall on their way to duty stations for shift rotation. They stopped and stood at attention as she exited her cabin, and she gave them a nod which set them back in motion.

She turned left, toward the *Regent Mary*'s bow, where the bridge lay—not on the bow, of course, but far enough away from both the engines and the ship's nose to offer some modicum of safety in battle.

That was what she liked about the *Mary*—she was a safe ship. Not the largest in her fleet, nor the most well-armed, but the safest. The *Mary* had seven layers to her hull, and every bulkhead bore additional reinforcement.

It wasn't that Krissy was a coward. Far from it. She had flown in a combat drop just last year. However, when she was commanding a fleet, when all those lives depended on her making the right call, then she wanted to be safe.

She climbed the ladders up two levels to the command deck, where she passed by the entrance to the CIC and her offices. There was nothing in either that demanded her attention at the moment—the bridge would be where she could best observe and control whatever happened next—which was hopefully nothing.

When Finaeus had arrived nine days ago, demanding access to the jump gate for a speedy return to Airtha, Krissy had wondered what his intentions really were—if there was one thing she knew about Finaeus, it was that he rarely revealed or stated his true goals—she had witnessed that first hand time and time again.

Nevertheless, whether she turned him away or sent him to Airtha—on his ship or hers—she needed to bring him down to Gisha. If for no other reason than to see him once more. Out of necessity—certainly not desire—she had also reported his arrival to the Admiralty.

She'd known they would be annoyed that the President's brother had finally reemerged, but to send in a Grey Division ship to pick him up? She had always suspected there was more to his exile than the brotherly spat born out of his crazy rantings.

Krissy stepped onto the bridge to a call of, "Admiral on the bridge," from the ship's XO, Major Nelson.

She noted the traditional straightening of backs and additional attentiveness that always came once the bridge crew spotted her arrival.

The *Mary* had a good crew, though sometimes its captain seemed less than professional. Such as now, when he wasn't present for their final approach.

"Major Nelson," Krissy nodded as she approached the command station near the back of the bridge.

"Admiral Krissy," Nelson replied, throwing her a quick salute. "We're t-minus ninety-three from port. There's a gravity-berm we have to ride, and then it will be smooth sailing the rest of the way to Gisha."

"Very good, Major Nelson," Krissy replied. "And where is Captain Lin?"

"He is in engineering, ma'am. The chief reported an issue in one of the cooling systems that required a reactor shutdown and he wanted to review the problem himself."

"Hmm," Krissy grunted. <*Hemdar, what is the status of the reactor?*>

Hemdar took her meaning and sent her confirmation that Captain Lin was indeed in engineering inspecting the reactor, while replying on the bridge net, <*We are at eighty-percent reactor capacity, CriEn's are untapped, and SC batts are fully charged. Nothing to worry about. We could kill all the burners and still pull into dock without trouble.*>

<*Thank you, Hemdar,*> Krissy replied.

Krissy stepped to the bridge's central holotank and pulled up a view of the ship they were spending all this effort on—the *Sabrina*.

If the ship had shown up without Finaeus aboard, she would have been tempted to blow it to dust and forget she had ever seen it, but Director Sera Tomlinson had passed orders that whoever found the *Sabrina* was to render whatever assistance it required—up to and including sending it to either Airtha, or New Canaan.

It created a lovely conflict of interest since New Canaan was an interdicted system and there was no way Krissy could allow a ship passage there, no matter what orders The Hand had passed down.

Luckily, Finaeus had asked for a jump to Airtha, which was much less problematic—if it weren't for the fact that he was in an Inner Stars vessel.

For starters, the *Sabrina* didn't even have the bow-mounted Ford-Svaiter mirror required to traverse the jump gate. They would have to retrofit one onto the freighter.

Which assumed that she could even allow such a thing to begin with. An Inner Stars ship gaining jump-gate tech and travelling to Airtha? To the heart of the Transcend? It was unheard of.

The intel on the ship indicated that it was crewed by smugglers and criminals that Sera had picked up during the years of her own exile. There was even a member of the interdicted New Canaan colony aboard—if reports were to be believed. No, there was almost no chance that this ship would ever reach Airtha.

Even less so now that a Grey Division ship was present.

As though he had read her mind, Major Nelson approached the holotank and spoke quietly to Krissy.

"Admiral, I assume you noticed the GD ship?"

Krissy nodded. "Yes, Stationmaster Lloyd saw fit to ruin my morning early and let me know about it."

"They're here for him, aren't they?" Nelson asked.

Krissy raised an eyebrow. "Either that, or me. Which do you think it is?"

The major appeared to not have expected such a caustic response and he nodded wordlessly.

"Someone doesn't want him to fly into Airtha on that freighter—which isn't a bad call—but if they think that Finaeus will willingly get on a GD ship, then they've another thing coming."

"How will he stop that from happening?" Nelson asked.

Krissy shook her head. "I have no idea, but if raw cunning ever took a physical form, it would be Finaeus."

<Admiral Krissy,> a voice entered her mind without requesting permission, and she knew who it was before reading the Link ident tag accompanying it.

<Colonel Bes,> she replied. *<How nice of you to visit us here at Grey Wolf. Are you in need of resupply, perhaps?>*

<I have orders to take Finaeus Tomlinson into custody and escort him to Airtha,> Bes replied.

<Orders? From whom? I have not received any orders yet.>

<You have now,> Bes said as he passed her an encrypted stream of data.

Krissy used her personal encryption key to unlock the authentication section of the data stream and read the order's source.

It simply read as originating from the Transcend's Admiralty, not from any specific person—just like every other order she had ever received from the Grey Division.

She reviewed the orders, and found that they were as she had suspected. Turn over Finaeus to Colonel Bes, extract the *Sabrina*'s AI, and then send all the humans and AI on the ship to Henover for interrogation.

That part at least made a bit more sense. Fleet Intel at Henover was a far better destination than the Greys. An addendum caught her eye. It noted that if Jessica Keller was indeed aboard the *Sabrina,* that she was to be sent along with Finaeus with Colonel Bes.

Back to wherever it was the Greys operated out of.

<I'll have to send a drone through the gate to confirm these orders,> Krissy replied. *<I will also handle Finaeus's extraction from the* Sabrina.*>*

<You have matching encryption keys, or you wouldn't be able to read those orders,> Bes replied, his tone clipped. *<You get him off the ship and then I'll take over from there.>*

*<***Colonel** *Bes. I suspect you forget who you are speaking with. I will do as I see fit in this matter. You will wait until I am satisfied with the veracity of every letter in these orders. Do I make myself clear?>*

She counted the seconds of silence before Bes replied. It came to fifteen.

<Yes, Admiral Krissy, I understand.>

<Good. I will meet you after we dock. Do not enter the Sabrina's *hangar under any circumstances. Am I clear?>*

<Crystal, Admiral.>

Krissy ended the communication and ran a hand through her short hair.

<Well, he's new at least,> Hemdar said.

<Yup, and just as self-important and annoying as the rest of them.>

<Do you think it was wise to antagonize him like that?>

Krissy wasn't sure, but there was no way she was going to let a colonel walk all over her. That was a short road to having one's command undermined.

She gave Hemdar a token response as she considered the addendum regarding Jessica Keller, the colonist woman.

The existence and location of the New Canaan colony was a well-kept secret. Even Krissy didn't know where it was—only that the GSS *Intrepid* had indeed met with the Transcend's Diplomatic Corps and been given a world in exchange for their advanced nanotech.

Which was something that still rankled her. Just their nanotech, not their cutting edge picotech, or their stasis shields.

She imagined what the Transcend fleets could do with stasis shields. The Orion Guard wouldn't last a decade with scale-tipping tech like that in the TSF's hands. She'd gladly lead the charge to chase them to the edge of the galaxy if need be.

Then they would finally have peace, the first since the FTL wars broke out five-thousand-years ago.

UNDERSTANDING

STELLAR DATE: 07.22.8938 (Adjusted Years)
LOCATION: ***Sabrina*****, Near Gisha Station**
REGION: DSM Ring, Grey Wolf System

"Until now, I had always wondered if the Transcend was a trick," Cargo said in a quiet voice.

"No trick," Finaeus replied. "As your eyes can attest."

Seeing the mining ring up close, Jessica had to agree. It was a thing of wonder—and they were still a quarter AU away.

The Grey Wolf's blueish light took on a much greyer hue as they drew closer to the elliptical plane. Clouds of carbon and oxygen flowed out from the star's surface, swirling in gravitational eddies formed by the orbiting black holes mounted in the ring wrapping around the star.

"How do you even build something like that?" Cheeky asked.

"Do you see any planets around here?" Finaeus smirked. "We tore them down to build the ring and create the mass for the first few black holes. Now there are thirty of them in there, all moving at a few thousand kilometers per second."

"Yeah, but how?" Cheeky asked. "You mined entire planets, and you said before that you've only been mining the star for a few hundred years."

"Oh, how do we make the *ring*? We put boosters on all the dwarf worlds in the system and smashed them into the system's two terrestrial worlds. That ejects a lot of material out into space. Out there we use magnetic fields to pull in the ferrous metals, and then charged ES fields to separate the rest. Then into the refineries.

"In the end, we smashed the two terrestrial worlds together to break them apart as much as possible. We built the orbital frames for the black holes, and then created the first few, feeding them the remains of the planets. Once the black holes had enough mass to balance out against hawking radiation loss, it was a simple matter of kicking them in toward the star in a close orbit. They tore off all the carbon we needed to complete the construction of the ring, and there you have it."

"Just like that," Jessica said with a laugh.

"You saw things like that back in Sol," Finaeus replied. "They did it with Neptune and Uranus. Pulled their clouds right off and fed them into Jupiter."

"That was before my time," Jessica shrugged. "By the time I was alive, Uranus's core was already in orbit of Jupiter, and Neptune was on its way to its new home in the Scattered Disk."

Finaeus shook his head. "Never understood that. Could have mixed it up just right, and fired a compressive antimatter blast around it...would have made a great super-Earth for InnerSol.

"Shows you how much clout Terra had lost by then. The Jovians happily sold it to the Scattered Worlds Alliance—and I guess we found out why," Cargo said.

Jessica nodded wordlessly. It was still difficult for her to think of what had happened to InnerSol at the hands of the Jovians. The only world they'd left habitable inside Ceres' orbit was Venus.

Five thousand years later, the Jovians had finally cleaned up Earth, but Luna and Mars were both still ruins, their once-great cities, broken and twisted reminders that the Jovians—now known as the Hegemony of Worlds—left for any who would test their might.

Jessica pushed the melancholic thoughts from her mind and focused on the growing form of Gisha Station.

A hub and spoke station, it was the tried and true style that had been in use for thousands of years. Even with inexpensive antimatter on hand, it was still more efficient to spin a station to simulate gravity than run AG systems everywhere.

The holodisplay noted that the station was over a hundred and fifty kilometers in diameter, with two-hundred and thirty-five ships in external berths on the outer ring. Many were easily recognizable as military vessels, though she spotted a small number of ships that appeared to be freighters—likely contractors that supplied the station with goods. Several large ships—nearly large enough to rival the Intrepid—were drifting near the station, likely undergoing refit and repair by the clouds of drones surrounding them.

As *Sabrina* approached, a new sight appeared in the distance; a one-thousand-kilometer long arch that was drawing in the clouds of material torn from the star, funneling it into two of the massive ships.

As they watched, one of the ships ceased its intake of material and a brilliant light erupted from it as antimatter-pion drives boosted the ship toward its destination—a ring several thousand kilometers retrograde off Gisha Station.

"The jump gate," Finaeus noted as he caught Jessica looking at it. "Getting these big daddies through a gate took a bit to work out. Focusing the negative energy across a ten-kilometer ring is no mean feat, but I solved it eventually."

<I'll never cease to be amazed that Finaeus, this rude, rather disheveled man, is the architect of so much of the Transend,> Iris commented privately.

<It certainly is incongruous,> Jessica agreed. *<However, he certainly is smart; he's fixed a dozen things on the ship that none of us even realized were broken. I did order Sabrina and Nance to keep him away from the stasis shields, though.>*

<I know, I've been assisting in that. He's really interested in how they work.>

<Probably just his insatiable curiosity, but still not something we can allow,> Jessica said

<*Yes, Tanis was very clear on that point.*>

"Jess, we've got a hail from one of the ships out there," Cheeky said from her station.

"Oh, shit, sorry, missed that," Jessica said, glancing down at her comm console. "Weird. It's from that smaller destroyer hanging out just off the outer docking ring over there."

Jessica glanced back to Cargo who nodded, and then placed the caller on the main holo tank.

The figure of a tall man resolved into view. His face was grim, and his brow was creased from a frown he must frequently wear. His long, dark hair fell behind his shoulder in tight curls. His grey uniform bore no markings other than a colonel's birds on his lapels.

"Captain Cargo, I am to inform you that your docking arrangements have been altered. Please alter course to dock with my ship and await further orders."

Cargo's frown deepened to match the man's. "Colonel…."

"Bes," the TSF officer supplied.

"Colonel Bes. I have very strict orders from a TSF admiral, and a berth from STC. If you would like to have those changed, please proceed through proper channels."

<*Kill it,*> Cargo said privately to Jessica, who all-too-happily complied before turning to Cargo.

"Cheery sort, wasn't he?"

"Kinda cute, though," Cheeky mused. "I'm OK with going to see him. Maybe I can get that frown off his face."

Jessica gave an appreciative laugh and leaned over to give the Cheeky a high-five.

"Friend of yours?" Cargo asked Finaeus, ignoring Cheeky's comment.

"Bes probably doesn't have any friends. He's GD."

"A Good Doobie?" Cheeky asked with a grin. "Doesn't seem like one to me."

"Grey Division. Officially known as the 137th Division of Space Force Strategic Research, but no one calls them that. They work for *her*," Finaeus replied.

"Her?" Cargo asked. "Any chance that's the same 'her' that President Tomlinson gave Airtha to?"

"One and the same," Finaeus grunted. "She was behind my exile as well—hunted me across the Inner Stars trying to take me out. I'd really hoped we would beat them down here. Fool's hope, I guess."

"Does she have a name?" Jessica asked.

"Jelina," Finaeus replied. "Whatever you do, don't dock with that ship."

"Wasn't planning on it," Cargo said. "You get a berth from a station, you take that berth. Especially when you can see their defense turrets tracking you."

Finaeus rubbed his jaw. "Maybe that was his hope. That we'd deviate and get blown away. Stuff like that is GD SOP."

"Well, I suspect that we'd get a warning first. Not really sure what his plan would be then," Cargo replied.

As he spoke scan lit up, registering beamfire, and Jessica hit the stasis shields an instant after Sabrina.

"What the—?" Cargo called out.

"Shit! That looks like it came from us!" Jessica exclaimed while re-running scan analysis on the shot.

Sure enough, analysis showed that the shot came from *Sabrina*'s forward dorsal beam. It had struck one of the nearby station turrets, tearing the unshielded weapon to shreds.

"Station's on comm," Jessica called out. "And surprise, surprise, that Bes guy just fired on us, tried to take out our engines, but Sabrina beat him to it with the shields."

"What a shit-show," Cargo grunted. "Put the station on."

"Vessel *Sabrina* what the hell was that! Why did you just fire on this station?" The call was audio only, and the voice was pissed.

"Gisha Station, this is Captain Cargo. I promise you, we did no such thing. Whatever just happened, that shot did not come from our ship."

"This is Stationmaster Lloyd. Our scan shows your dorsal weapon hot, and now you have shields up."

"I don't understand it yet, either," Cargo replied calmly. "But we raised shields because we thought we were under attack, and it's good that we did because that Colonel Bes guy just shot at us."

There was no response from Stationmaster Lloyd, and a new call came in. "It's our friend, the Admiral," Jessica said.

Cargo sighed and waved his hand. "Let's see what she has to say."

"Captain Cargo," Admiral Krissy said, her expression severe. "You've just made my day immeasurably worse. Thank you very much."

"I assure you, we did not fire. And we were fired upon," Cargo insisted.

"That's not what our logs show. You clearly took out that target and raised shields. Despite your protestations to Stationmaster Lloyd, we have no records of any ship firing upon yours."

"Funny that this all happened right after Colonel Bes instructed us to change course to dock with his ship," Finaeus said. "Don't be daft, Krissy. This is the GD's modus operandi through and through. What do we have to gain from an attack on Gisha? We need your cooperation. He wants us dead. Or worse."

"Is this more of your insane ramblings…Finaeus? Nonsense like this is what got you kicked out of Huygens all those years ago. It's time you put all that aside." Admiral Krissy appeared as though she was going to say more, but then stopped and shook her head. "We're running a detailed analysis on the attack, but if the scan data holds up, we're going to have to take you into custody. You can't just fire on a TSF facility and get away with it."

"FGT, Krissy. This is an FGT facility. I've been away for a while, but Stationmaster Lloyd isn't military, and neither is Gisha," Finaeus countered.

"Close enough as to make no matter, these days, Finaeus. Now, Captain Cargo. Lower your shields and prepare to be boarded. This little game has come to an end."

"Cheeky, take us out of here," Cargo ordered.

"You got it, Captain, New Canaan, here we come," Cheeky called out triumphantly

Jessica killed the connection to Admiral Krissy and glanced back at Cargo. "I assume you were done with her."

<*I sure am,*> Sabrina said. <*Any station that shoots at us is on my naughty list. I don't dock at naughty stations.*>

"Weak, Sabs," Cheeky said. "We live for naughty stations. You need to work at metaphors and allegory more."

<*Trying.*>

<*They must have a stealth ship around here,*> Iris said. <*I bet it was right on top of us and shot at the station; then fired a beam at our dorsal weapons to heat them up. It's the only explanation that makes sense.*>

Finaeus stroked his chin. "Yes, yes, that would work. You have many upgrades from the *Intrepid,* but not a sensor suite that could detect a stealthed TSF vessel. Especially not a GD ship. But how did the GD sneak one in under Krissy's nose?"

"You better find out, because we're not going anywhere," Cheeky said.

"What do you mean?" Cargo asked.

"Station here has some serious grav emitters. They're pulling us back. I could fire up the AP drive, or the burners, but we're inside their shields. We'll kill everyone on the station."

"Fuck!" Cargo swore.

"That's one hell of a gamble they're taking," Jessica said.

"There's another layer of shielding that would keep them safe...provided you didn't run your AP's at max. Point-blank focused gamma rays would melt any organics in their path," Finaeus said.

"The admiral's betting on our decency, then, is she?" Cargo asked. "A bit risky with a bunch of Inner Stars smugglers like us."

"Or they think they can take out our stasis shields," Jessica suggested. "They have had some time to study what we did back at Bollam's."

Cargo pushed the heels of his hands into his eyes and sighed. "Put the admiral back on."

"Captain Cargo," Admiral Krissy said as she appeared with a frown and crossed arms on the holotank. "I assume you've thought better of your folly? You're not leaving."

"No," Cargo replied. "But only because we're not murderers. We'll come in, but we'll take the dock you offered. We're not leaving *Sabrina* out here where Bes can take more pot shots at it with his stealthed ship."

Jessica noted that Krissy's eyes widened slightly, and then narrowed before she replied. "Very well, but power your reactors down."

UNCERTAINTY

STELLAR DATE: 07.22.8938 (Adjusted Years)
LOCATION: TSS *Regent Mary*, Near Gisha Station
REGION: DSM Ring, Grey Wolf System

"Is that possible?" Captain Lin asked in a low voice. "Could they have brought a stealthed ship with them?"

Krissy let out a long breath. It certainly wasn't possible to hide a stealth ship in Grey Wolf for long. Bending photons and rads around a ship was one thing, but eventually its silhouette would stand out against the ever-shifting grav fields.

That meant if there was one, it jumped in right on the tail of Bes's destroyer—though she had never heard of a ship jumping in stealth before.

"Have your teams review scan again," Krissy said. "Look at everything for the past two hours. I want to know definitively whether or not there's a stealth ship in Grey Wolf."

"Yes, ma'am," Captain Lin said, before looking to Nelson.

Krissy held back a comment. Once Lin had been a good captain, but for some reason his heart just wasn't in it anymore. If war wasn't looming, she'd recommend retirement for him.

It certainly wasn't fair to Nelson—not that fair was the goal—but she didn't want to ruin a good officer by saddling him with the duties, but not the honor, of a captain.

One crisis at a time. Lin could muddle through for a bit longer.

<*Colonel Bes,*> she called the Grey Division officer.

The reply was instantaneous. <*Admiral Krissy, quite the mess you have on your hands.*>

<*Finaeus and the crew of the* Sabrina *would have me believe you were responsible. They have claimed that you fired upon them and that there must be a stealthed ship present.*>

Bes snorted. <*Likely story. Allow me to take custody of Finaeus and the colony woman and we'll relieve you of this headache.*>

<*I have still not received confirmation of your orders,*> Krissy replied. <*And I'm inclined to take their argument seriously. I can't think of any reason why they'd fire on the station just once.*>

<*They're rogues. Pirates from a backwater corner of the Inner Stars. Why they do anything is a mystery. Maybe they were just testing our resolve. Maybe they have a trigger-happy gunner. Either way, there is protocol to be followed. You must take them into custody, and then my claim supersedes yours.*>

Krissy chewed on the inside of her cheek, biting back what she wanted to say to Bes. Chances were that Finaeus was right, but without any proof, there would be little she could do. Once those orders were confirmed she would have no choice but to comply with Bes's demands.

She considered letting the *Sabrina* go. All she had to do was order Lloyd to turn off the grav field holding the freighter in place. He would probably comply—he had no desire to take that ship into his station.

But that would go badly for her—though not as badly as it would for Finaeus and the crew of the *Sabrina*.

No, this would have to play out a little longer.

<*Dock,*> she ordered Bes. <*I'll speak to you in person once we're both on Gisha.*>

"Anything?" she addressed Captain Lin, though her eyes looked to Major Nelson.

"Nothing," Nelson replied. "We'll keep looking, but scan is clean. No signatures at all. No sensor suite in the fleet, or on Gisha, picked up a shot from Bes's ship either."

Krissy nodded absently. "Picking up the beam would be hard, unless you were looking for it—but we'd see the ionized atoms. Space isn't exactly empty around here."

"Yes, Admiral," Nelson agreed. "A lot of dust about. We'd see the trail."

"Very well," Krissy said. "Bring us in. I want to be there to meet Finaeus when he disembarks."

<What are you going to do?> Hemdar asked.

<Probably something I'll regret before long.>

GISHA STATION

STELLAR DATE: 07.22.8938 (Adjusted Years)
LOCATION: *Sabrina*, Gisha Station
REGION: DSM Ring, Grey Wolf System

"Aaand we're in the cradle," Cheeky reported.

"This stinks," Cargo said. "Any ideas what our next move should be?"

"We have to get out of here as quickly as possible," Finaeus said. "That GD commander won't have any of our best interests at heart."

"We're not going anywhere with that grav field there," Cheeky said. "Not unless you're willing to kill everyone on this station…"

"If it comes down to them or us, that'll be an option I'll consider," Cargo said. "But for now, I'll meet with them and see if we can't resolve this peacefully."

"Not on your own, you're not," Jessica said. "You need backup. Besides, I'll bet Finaeus has something up his sleeve that Iris can use to disable their grav field."

"What makes you think I have something like that?" Finaeus asked.

<*Because you keep going on and on about how you're the genius behind all this,*> Sabrina said. <*Now it's time for you to put your money where your mouth is and get us out of this jam that you got us into in the first place.*>

"Oh, well, I can see how you'd think that…" Finaeus said.

"So?" Jessica asked.

"So what?" Finaeus asked back.

Cargo rose from his seat and approached Finaeus. "What do you have up your sleeve, old man? Time's running short. There's a whole lot of troops forming up around us out there."

Jessica hadn't looked at the exterior views, and when she checked she saw that Cargo wasn't exaggerating. There were at least a hundred TSF soldiers in the bay. They were setting up defensive shields and heavy weapons all around *Sabrina*.

<*I'm not worried. I still have the stasis shields on—except for around the base of the cradle, but they'd have to crawl right under us to get a shot in there,*> Sabrina said.

"No problem," Finaeus said as he altered the view on the bridge holotank. "There's Krissy walking into the bay. I'll just go down and talk to her and—"

"Seriously, Fin," Jessica shook her head. "For some sort of big smart guy, you're damn stupid. They want *you* most of all. I'll go out and see what we can work out."

"Correction," Cargo said. "We'll go out. Sabrina, if we're not back in twelve hours, and everything isn't all hunky-dory, you fire up the AP drive and blast your way out of this joint. I don't care who gets fried. Sera wants Finaeus delivered to New Canaan and she'll get him."

"OK," Jessica said. "Then here's the plan…"

*****

"This is a horrible plan," Jessica muttered as the ship's airlock cycled. "We've had some dumb plans over the years, but this is the worst…the absolute worst."

"Jess, it's your plan, have a little faith in yourself," Cargo replied.

"I thought someone would come up with a better plan! This was supposed to be the starter plan…the one that got the juices flowing. Not *the* plan."

"I guess you're just a strategic genius," Cargo chuckled.

"Go me," she replied as the pressure equalization light turned green and the outer lock door began to open.

She glanced to Cargo, who wore a sharp uniform, and then to her own outfit, a tight blue one-piece suit that Trevor had picked up for her a few systems back. It was a favorite of his because he liked that it set off her skin and hair.

Probably not the most conservative thing to meet the Transcend's admiral in, but it was what she had on, and there was no time to change.

<You never know,> Iris said. *<Between Krissy and Bes, the odds are that one of them likes girls. It may work to your advantage.>*

<Gotta use what you're born with—or in my case, what the job set you up with.>

Even so, she hated being at a disadvantage, and something about Krissy led her to believe that Jessica's mode of dress may lower her value in the other woman's eyes.

<I can't read your mind, but I can tell you're nervous. Use it. She's going to underestimate you. That's a good thing,> Iris said.

<Thanks Iris, you're right. I used to do this sort of thing all the time—I got this.>

<That's right, you got this.>

The airlock door slid aside and revealed the muzzles of sixty guns pointed at them. The weapons—and the soldiers holding them—were on the far side of the stasis shield, but it still felt damn disconcerting.

In their midst, stood Admiral Krissy, alone, a look of grim displeasure on her face.

<No sycophants,> Cargo noted. *<She's gonna be a tough nut to crack. No angles to play with subordinates.>*

<AI here are not chatty either,> Hank added. *<They seem…strange.>*

Jessica filed that away for future consideration as they approached the woman.

"Here goes," she whispered as the stasis shield opened enough for them to step through.

"Welcome to Gisha Station," Admiral Krissy said as they approached. She walked forward to meet them, but did not offer her hand.

"Thank you, though the welcome seems strained," Cargo replied, glancing at the soldiers filling the docking bay.

"You did fire on this station," Krissy said. "I cannot ignore that fact."

"And I tell you that we did no such thing. Our logs show that our weapons were offline, and we provided them to your STC immediately," Cargo responded. "There is no logical reason that would cause us to fire on you."

"So you say, but we have to trust our own sensors, and they do not back your story."

The woman paused, and Jessica waited for the hammer to fall.

"I am placing you under arrest for violating the sovereignty of the Transcend Interstellar Alliance, and firing on one of the FGT's installations during a time of war."

"Wow," Jessica muttered. "And I assume that's a war crime on your books?"

Krissy nodded. "It is. My hands are tied here. Our laws are very strict when it comes to the FGT. We brook no violence toward them."

"How very noble of you," Cargo replied. "So, what's next? The hot irons? Needles? Trust me, you're not going to crack us, or the shell around our ship."

"We'll see about that," Krissy replied. She turned, and eight TSF soldiers approached with weapons leveled. Jessica looked to Cargo, sighed, and held out her hands.

<OK, already on to plan B.>

* * * * *

"Think we'll be meeting with that Colonel Bes before long?" Jessica asked as she and Cargo sat in a small conference room.

She was surprised that they hadn't been separated. Perhaps Admiral Krissy wasn't fully onboard with what was going on and wasn't going to make things any easier for the Grey Division man.

"Probably. I hope so. Room service here sucks," Cargo replied. "Would it kill you guys to bring in some coffee?" he hollered at the closed door.

<*What's your status,*> she asked Iris and Hank.

<*They have some exceptional suppression tech in here,*> Hank replied.

<*Just one level below that EMP that fight club smoked us with back on Chittering Hawk,*> Iris added. <*But I've worked up a few tricks since then. Not going to be disabled like that a second time.*>

<*So you're confident that the hackit you dropped in the docking bay will make it here?*> Hank asked. <*Because we can't talk to anything outside this room.*>

<*Well…I sure hope it will,*> Iris smirked. <*If it doesn't we're totally screwed.*>

<*There's still plan C,*> Cargo said.

<*What, the plan that has* Sabrina *blasting out of here and cooking us all?*> Hank asked

<*No, that's plan F,*> Iris replied.

<*I still don't get why they let us dock in here. It really doesn't make sense. We're not decent folk. We could have fried them.*> Cargo said.

As they were speaking, the door opened, and Admiral Krissy entered, still alone—something Jessica had not expected.

She gave both of them a long look before sitting down at the table.

"Smart move leaving Finaeus in there," she said. "Bes would have snatched him up so fast that I wouldn't have had any time to explore other options."

"Don't see eye to eye with your friends in the 137th?" Cargo asked.

Krissy gave a rueful laugh. "I see Finaeus has been sharing details. Yes, the Grey Division and most of the TSF do not see eye-to-eye. Bes wants you too by the way," Krissy said with a nod to Jessica.

"Who? Little ol' me?" Jessica asked with mock innocence.

"Yes, you, Jessica Keller, born in Athabasca, District of Saskatchewan, the year four-thousand and fifty-two on the old Gregorian calendars. You joined the Terran Bureau of Investigations when you were twenty-six and graduated with honors from their training facility in Rio de Janeiro in the year four-thousand and eighty-two. After that you were stationed in High Terra, though there are a few sections of your record that are blank—likely classified at the time and never made it to us."

"Wow!" Jessica exclaimed with a clap of her hands. "You just know all about me, now, don't you? Should we move next into a little game where we show off our powers of observation to one another? Nit about small stains and eyebrow hairs out of place and surmise life-traits from those? It could pass the time while you wait to see of Bes's orders are valid; before you have to turn Finaeus over to him—which you don't want to do because our quirky old man means something to you, and you to him. Or you wouldn't have let our ship dock in the station," Jessica paused, gauging Krissy's reactions. "You really have no reason to fear that he'll blast his way out of here, do you?"

A small smile pulled at the edges of Admiral Krissy's lips. "So you *are* smarter than you look. I'd hoped so."

"Why's that?" Cargo asked.

"Because Bes's orders are validated, and he's coming here to collect you," Krissy replied. "I don't know who approved them, but it has all the right tokens. There's nothing I can do."

"Funny that I'm top of mind for him," Jessica said.

"Yes, the Grey Division wants you almost as much as they want Finaeus, though I don't quite know what has piqued their interest so much. Perhaps they think you know something useful about the *Intrepid*'s picotech."

"They'd be disappointed," Jessica replied. "That's above my pay grade."

"And the rest of us?" Cargo asked.

Krissy shrugged. "Standard containment procedures."

"That doesn't sound promising," Cargo said.

"Conditioning if you'll take it, incarceration if you won't—or if the conditioning doesn't take."

<*And us?*> Hank asked.

"The same," Krissy replied nonchalantly.

"So, what's our play," Cargo asked Jessica. "Think if we take her we can use her as a hostage?"

"Not against Bes, that guy probably doesn't give a rat's ass about Krissy here. But if we can get the word out to her fleet, they may feel differently."

"We don't negotiate with hostage takers," Krissy replied amicably, "Though I would like to think that my fleet would try something to save me. Hard to say, though."

"You seem unconcerned with the turn this conversation has taken," Cargo said.

Krissy shrugged. "I knew what I was getting into when I came in here alone. I won't be complicit in anything. I believe in the Transcend, but I don't believe in Bes and his Greys. And I'm certainly not going to sacrifice Finaeus on their alter. Just make sure it's nothing too damaging."

"Do you have an AI?" Jessica asked.

"No, I'm currently between AI," Krissy replied.

"Good, that will make this simpler."

Jessica's restraints fell from her limbs and she lunged across the table, grabbing Krissy's throat with one hand, and placing another on the base of her skull.

The admiral put up a good fight, and Jessica took an elbow to the face, then another to her throat."

"Fuck!" Jessica screamed as Krissy almost wrenched free, and then Cargo was there, his strong arms holding the admiral in place as Jessica finally managed to get her finger on Krissy's hard-Link port.

A moment later the Admiral went limp.

"Well that was easy," Jessica said.

<*She let me in,*> Iris replied. <*Had an encryption hash in a file on her public net. I made it look like she put up a fight, but I didn't have to do anything brutal.*>

"I sure hope that part of this little ruse she set up involved fooling the room sensors for a bit," Cargo said.

"Had to, or we'd be neck-deep in soldiers by now," Jessica replied.

Jessica quickly stripped out of her clothing as Cargo undressed the Admiral. Four minutes later she was doing up the last button on the rather uncomfortable formal jacket Krissy wore as Cargo was settling Krissy down in Jessica's seat, placing the restraints back around her wrists.

"Trevor's going to be pissed that I lost that outfit," she sighed

Cargo glanced up at her. "Yeah, that uniform's a poor substitute. Barely makes it around your hips."

"Yeah, maybe it's time that I tried out a regular physique again," Jessica replied as she attempted to get the jacket to hang properly over her narrow waist.

"Nah, you love being you," Cargo chuckled. "Besides, having you around makes Cheeky feel more comfortable with being who she is."

Jessica shrugged as she took her seat. She adjusted her jacket once more before shaking her head, triggering her long lavender locks to match Krissy's light brown hair, thankful that she had picked up a hair-color mod after Iris kept making her grays fall out.

Maybe getting a mod to change skin color on demand should be next on her list. Every now and then it *was* useful to blend in.

Still, she didn't need the disguise to last for long, just a few seconds to fool whoever came in next.

SABRINA BESIEGED

STELLAR DATE: 07.22.8938 (Adjusted Years)
LOCATION: *Sabrina*, Docking Bay F34A Gisha Station
REGION: DSM Ring, Grey Wolf System

"Who'd have thought," Cheeky said around a mouthful of almonds, "that when Sera recruited us years ago, we'd be pulling off crazy jobs like this—trying to steal wormhole tech from a mythical civilization we all thought was long gone."

"Certainly not me," Nance said from across the galley table, wearing her best hazsuit with the hood pulled off so she could eat. "Granted, I never really expected to spend any appreciable time out of a hazsuit either, so I've already had some life-altering changes."

<*Or me finding freedom,*> Piya added.

<*I still can't believe I volunteered for this,*> Erin said with a laugh.

"Hey!" Nance exclaimed

<*I'm kidding, Nance,*> Erin said, her tone mollifying. <*I joined up because I got too much of a taste for adventure during the* Intrepid*'s journey. I wasn't ready to settle down in some colony job, or while away my years in an expanse.*>

"I thought Tanis just ordered you to join up," Cheeky said.

<*You'd think that, wouldn't you?*> Erin chuckled.

No one spoke for a minute, and Cheeky rose to brew a fresh pot of coffee.

Once the glorious black liquid began to drip into the pot—an archaic, but delicious way to brew it—she turned and looked at Nance who was still sitting at the table, staring into the distance.

"Think about Thompson much?" Cheeky asked.

Nance let out a long sigh before pushing her long, brown hair aside to look at Cheeky.

"Every damn day. That bastard…after all that time. I thought we really had something. I guess I was just a convenient fuck or something."

"Nance! Don't you let me catch you placing one iota of your self-worth in the hands of Thompson. Sure, he was crew, but he was always a self-centered ass," Cheeky said, wanting to walk over to Nance and give the woman a hug.

She didn't, though. Even after all these years, Nance still wasn't big on physical contact. Especially when she was feeling out of sorts.

Nance swallowed and shook her head. "I'm not…at least I think I'm not. It's more that I thought maybe we could build a life together. You know, settle down somewhere. It didn't have to be New Canaan, I would have been OK with somewhere else…."

<*It takes a bit,*> Erin said. <*You haven't adjusted to thinking of a future without him yet.*>

"Thanks Erin, but I don't think that I need relationship advice from an AI," Nance grumbled.

<*Hey, I know you're upset, but I'm just trying to help. I've been inside more human heads than you have. I may know a few things about coping—not to mention we AI have similar issues from time to time,*> Erin replied.

"You do?" Cheeky asked, sorry that she had started this conversation, and eager for an opportunity to change the topic. "I didn't think AI formed any sort of long-term partnership."

<*We have our own flavors of it,*> Erin replied. <*Sometimes we blend parts of our minds with others, either temporarily, or in a way that permanently alters us—sort of a second birth in that case. Sometimes…well…sometimes we don't like what we see in one another. Sometimes we fall away and don't communicate anymore.*>

"Doesn't seem that different from human relationships," Cheeky said. "The second part, at least."

<*That was my point,*> Erin replied.

Heavy footsteps echoed down the passageway, and a moment later Trevor entered the galley and fell into a chair.

"Any word?" he asked.

"Nope," Cheeky shook her head. "Not that we expected to hear anything this early on."

"Sure is a crazy plan—one of our daringest…is that a word?" Nance added. "They go off, get captured—hoping it will lead them to getting a hackit in place—and we just sit here, waiting to see if those soldiers out there try to blow a hole in *Sabrina*."

"I suppose it could be worse," Trevor said with a shrug. "We could be in a ship without stasis shields."

<*You may be before long,*> Sabrina said. <*SC Batt number three just blew a cooling loop. It's losing charge fast.*>

<*Well, shit,*> Piya swore.

"We can't just run the reactor?" Trevor asked.

"Inside a stasis shield, inside a station?" Cheeky responded. "We've nowhere to vent our heat. We'd bake."

Trevor grinned and gestured at the soldiers in the bay, visible on one of the displays in the galley. "Yeah, but so would they. Bottom of the ship isn't shielded. I bet we could use the grav drives to gently waft heat out of there."

<*It wouldn't work fast enough,*> Sabrina said. <*We'd cook in here long before we could vent enough heat out there. Plus, the bay's not that big, it wouldn't buy us much more time.*>

"Ideas?" Cheeky asked. "Once that shield goes down, those nice men and women out there are going to come knocking."

"We could shoot out the bay doors and vent our heat into space," Nance suggested. "Sure, they won't like it, but they are pointing guns at us."

<*Well, maybe we could run the fusion reactor really low and slow, and keep the stasis shields powered at their minimal level. We'll*

save the remaining charge on the SC Batts for when we need it,> Sabrina suggested.

<*I thought you said it would get too hot in here.*> Piya said. <*Not that I care too much, but Cheeky gets grumpy when she's hot.*>

"Who doesn't?" Cheeky asked

"I think it could work," Nance said. "If we do the smaller, secondary reactor, and vent the heat out the dorsal vanes. It would make it a lot less comfortable for them than for us—at least for a bit. We'd have to vent it out the top, though."

"How long's a bit?" Trevor asked.

<*Three, maybe four hours,*> Sabrina replied.

<*I don't know about this,*> Piya said nervously.

"Relax," Cheeky said to her AI. "With SC Batts one and two we can run the shield for hours after it gets too hot from the reactor."

<*Oh dear,*> Sabrina said.

"What now? You couldn't even have the reactor warm yet," Cheeky said.

<*No, but I think we're being boarded,*> Sabrina replied.

"What?" several voices called out at once.

<*Hmm…maybe…nope—definitely being boarded. One group just got the port-side airlock open, and the other has come through the maintenance hatch under environmental.*>

"I blame you, Trevor," Nance said. "You jinxed us earlier when you mentioned that."

"Me?"

Finaeus raced into the galley, far faster than Cheeky would have expected an older man to manage.

"Sabrina pinged me. I assume you have weapons on this pirate ship? Other than what you all usually carry around."

Cheeky passed him on her way in the corridor. "Of course we do, and we're not a pirate ship. Follow me to the weapons stash. Nance, get to the bridge, help co-ordinate from there.

Trevor, you're going to take environmental, Finaeus and I will take the port-side airlock."

"I'm not holing up on the bridge," Nance argued as she ran into the passageway and matched speed with Cheeky. "I'm going with Trevor to environmental. I can kill those guys six ways from flag day down there without ever firing a shot."

"Fine," Cheeky nodded. "Just...only take a pulse rifle. I've seen you shoot."

At the end of the corridor, Cheeky slid aside a panel, revealing an array of weapons. They ranged from a pair of ballistic pistols to beam rifles. She passed on those weapons and handed out four multifunction weapons, capable of firing pulses, and low-velocity projectiles.

"These aren't going to do much good," Trevor said. "If they're wearing armor—which I'm sure they will be—we're going to need beams or plasma."

<No one's firing plasma in me!> Sabrina exclaimed. *<You can do high-powered kinetics or x-ray lasers if you're careful.>*

"Fine," Cheeky said and everyone quickly swapped rifles. "Now go! We don't have much time."

Trevor and Nance slid down the ladder to the cargo deck and then one level further to environmental and engineering. Cheeky gave Finaeus a level look. "You know how to shoot that thing?"

"I think I can figure it out," Finaeus replied. "Pointy end goes toward the bad guys, right?"

"Har, har," Cheeky said as she slid down the ladder to the cargo deck. It annoyed her that she let Nance bully her into wearing clothes—just in case they had to meet with someone formal, she'd said. Armor was one thing, but clothes just got in the way of most things.

She and Sera had always seen eye-to-eye on that.

"You go there," she directed Finaeus to a position behind a conduit stack in the port-side corridor. "I'll be down on the far side of the airlock. We'll catch them in the crossfire."

"Just don't shoot me," Finaeus said as he took the position and leveled his rifle at the airlock door."

"We've practiced this a lot," Cheeky said as she ran down to a crate on the far side of the airlock—left there for just this reason.

"Sera had you drilling, did she?" Finaeus asked.

Cheeky smiled as she took aim on the airlock. "All the time. Cargo's made us keep it up too."

<They haven't managed to crack our upgraded security on the airlock's inner door. I think they're just going to cut through it,> Sabrina advised.

<Open it, and give them the welcome, then,> Cheeky said. *<No reason to hose a perfectly good lock.>*

<Setting a timer on your HUD,> Sabrina said.

Cheeky saw a five-second-countdown appear over her vision. She braced against the wall and clenched her teeth, forcing herself to take deep breaths and ignore the possibility that they could be her last.

The timer hit zero and the doors slid open.

She pulled up the corridor's camera feeds and saw seven soldiers in medium-powered armor—tough stuff, but still slim enough to get through a freighter's passageways and hatches.

Cheeky counted slowly, waiting for the first of the Transcend soldiers to move into the passageway—something they appeared hesitant to do—all too aware that they weren't the ones who had opened the door.

<A smart person would run,> Piya said. *<An airlock is a shitty place to be trapped. They have to know we're waiting for them.>*

<No kidding,> Cheeky replied.

Sera had always told them that the best thing to do if someone got into your airlock, was not to let them out. The ideal scenario option was to drop a concussive blast into the lock while they were cycling it.

To that end, each airlock on *Sabrina* had murder holes in the overhead and bulkheads that would drop conc grenades on unsuspecting intruders, but these soldiers weren't some gang on a run-down station. Their first order of business had been to set up a grav shield that would protect them from just such an attack.

Now, if she were in their shoes—something that Sera had also trained them on—she would be tossing something unpleasant out in to the corridor right smartly.

On cue, two of the soldiers tossed a pair of grenades into the passageway, aiming for Cheeky and Finaeus's positions.

Except the grenades didn't enter the corridor.

The instant the enemy soldiers released the grenades, a stasis shield snapped down over the airlock entrance and the explosives bounced back inside.

<*Duck!*> Sabrina called out, and Cheeky crouched low behind her crate.

The concussive blast roared out into the corridor and rattled Cheeky's teeth.

<*Sorry,*> Sabrina said. <*I did the math and those 'nades were going to crack the hull if I didn't let the excess force out…though it wasn't as much energy as I'd predicted…something's off.*>

<*Felt like plenty of force here,*> Finaeus grunted.

The smoked cleared out of the airlock, and Cheeky saw that two soldiers were down, and three appeared disoriented with weapons lowered.

The final two were still in position at the edges of the airlock, ready to line up shots.

<*They have probes out, they can see you as well as you can see them,*> Sabrina warned.

"Shit!" Cheeky exclaimed, and ducked back as a pulse blast slammed into her crate. Luckily, the thing wasn't just an empty box, but a dense grav shield.

A grav shield that reflected the man's pulse back onto him.

"We're gonna be a tough nut to crack!" Cheeky called out. "Why don't you little 'Scenders just go back home and tell mom and dad that we can't come out to play."

"You can't hold out forever," one of the soldiers called back. "Surrender now and save yourself a world of trouble."

"No chance," Cheeky called back. "What you didn't count on is how much I like trouble." She completed the statement by blowing a kiss.

<You just can't turn it off, can you?> Finaeus asked.

<Turn what off?> Cheeky replied.

More concussive shots came out of the airlock. Cheeky and Finaeus returned fire, sticking to the x-ray lasers—kinetics were out of the question without clear targets.

<They're trying to slip a hack past one of your maintenance routines,> Finaeus said to Sabrina. *<Check the main cargo bay's subnet.>*

<Holy crap! I didn't notice that. How did you spot it?> Sabrina said.

<I'm not just a pretty face,> Finaeus replied as he took another shot at one of the Transcend soldiers that had leaned just a bit too far out of the airlock.

<OK, I've locked it down,> Sabrina said. *<I think they might try to try to cut through the door, though.>*

<This is getting ridiculous,> Cheeky said. *<There are grenades in the main weapons lockup. You hold them here, Fin. I'm going to go get them.>*

<Are you kidding?> Finaeus exclaimed. *<If you leave, and there's no crossfire, they'll overrun me.>*

<Think so?> Cheeky asked.

<Yes, I think so!>

<I think you've been in more battles than you let on.>

<If you guys could finish up there, we'd sure love some help down here,> Trever said. *<They got a whole squad in environmental. Nance flushed something nasty out of some of the tanks and its slowing them down, but they're still coming.>*

<Ewww…Nance, what did you do?> Cheeky asked

<Something I'm going to hate cleaning up later,> Nance replied with a rueful laugh. *<Nothing corrosive, but it did force them all to switch over to internal air supplies.>*

<I really don't want to know—and I'm never coming back down there—> Cheeky said.

<Seriously, help!> Trever interrupted.

<'Kay, Fin, on the count of three, we rush 'em. Sabrina, do the gravity thing,> Cheeky said.

<I guess this is as good as our planning's going to get, isn't it?> Piya said.

Cheeky didn't reply, but the next time the Transcend soldiers pulled back into cover, she jumped out from behind her cover and charged toward the airlock.

As they rushed forward, Sabrina reversed the grav systems in the lock and down became up.

The unconscious soldiers fell to the overhead, as did two of the conscious ones. The final two had their boots mag-locked to the deck, but suddenly found themselves hanging from the ceiling.

Cheeky fired a short burst of kinetic rounds at the pelvis of the one closest to her—almost always the weakest spot—while Finaeus fired center-mass at the other.

The rounds cracked, then penetrated their armor. Cheeky fired a few more rounds into the soldiers lying on the airlock's overhead for good measure.

"Surrender. Now!"

The two who had taken the initial rounds had already dropped their weapons, and the others—those who could—followed suit.

"I'm going to open the outer lock, and you ass-hats are going to take your wounded and get the fuck off our ship."

<*Uh…Cheeky?*> Sabrina asked.

<*What?*>

<*The outer lock is open already.*>

Cheeky looked at the outer lock—which was securely closed. She could see it plainly.

<*I can see it. It's closed.*>

<*It's a really good holo. Fooled my sensors for a bit too—its why the grenades didn't do enough damage. Their force went out into the bay.*>

Cheeky suddenly felt very vulnerable, knowing that there could be a whole squad of enemy troops on the other side of the airlock.

<*Well, not that many,*> Piya said. <*They have to climb up here, and there's not much room between the ship and the shield.*>

A second later, the holo disappeared and Cheeky saw two more enemies outside the ship—but within the stasis shield—taking aim. She ducked behind one of the soldiers who still hung—or stood, depending on your point of view—by his mag-locked boots.

Finaeus wasn't as fast, and cried out as a pulse blast hit him.

"I'm OK…mostly," he grunted a moment later.

Cheeky sprayed rounds out of the airlock door and winced as they bounced off the inside of the stasis shield, some hitting the hull, and others coming back through the airlock. More than one passing far too close to her head.

<*Careful!*> Piya admonished.

<You're telling me,> Cheeky said privately before calling out, "I'm going to hole every one of your buddies in here if you don't back the fuck off!"

"You wouldn't!" a voice called back from outside the ship.

"Wanna find out?" Cheeky asked and fired another round out the airlock, this one aimed to bounce off the shield and hit somewhere close to where the speaker's voice originated.

"Shit! OK, OK. Let us come in to get our wounded. We're dropping our weapons."

"Deal," Cheeky replied. *<Fin, get down below, see if you can help. I can take care of this from here.>*

<What if they rush you?>

<Sabrina can still snap on the inner stasis field.>

Cheeky knew that wasn't a great solution. The airlock's inner stasis field's emitters were vulnerable from inside the airlock, but it would stop any funny business.

She hoped.

COLONEL BES

STELLAR DATE: 07.22.8938 (Adjusted Years)
LOCATION: Interrogation Room, Gisha Station
REGION: DSM Ring, Grey Wolf System

Jessica had just settled into the seat previously held by Admiral Krissy when she heard the door open behind her and Bes's voice call out.

"So, still having your chat, Krissy? You know that there's nothing you can do now."

Jessica waited for Bes to step into the room, and smiled at the sound of the door closing behind him. He was alone.

The colonel reached for the chair beside her, and Jessica rose and spun, driving a fist in the underside of his jaw. Bes's teeth snapped together, and she hoped a few broke, as he fell backward.

Unlike Admiral Krissy, Bes was armed and Jessica knew controlling that weapon—or at least getting it out of play—was key. She steeled herself for what would occur when she touched his sidearm, and reached out to grab it.

Her hand clamped around the weapon's grip and she cried out as it discharged a shock into her body, though she still managed to wrench it free of its holster.

By the time she had fallen to the floor, hand still convulsively clenched around the handgun, Cargo was on top of Bes.

The Grey Division colonel had recovered from Jessica's initial blow and was holding his own against Cargo. *Sabrina*'s captain was a tough man, a veteran of a hundred dock-side fights and bar brawls, but Bes was a trained soldier who was also heavily augmented.

For every solid hit Cargo delivered, Bes delivered two, and from the looks of it, they hurt a lot.

<*Can you wipe his DNA lock on the handgun?*> Jessica asked Iris as she struggled to her feet.

<*Working on it, almost—damn. It just fried itself. Sorry.*>

<*No problem,*> Jessica said as she flexed her right hand. Had she possessed organic skin the weapon's bio-lock would have severely burned her flesh. As it was, the polymers that made up her epidermis were just a bit melted.

"Hey, Bes," she said. "You want me? Come and get me."

Bes delivered punch to Cargo's solar plexus that sent the captain reeling before turning to Jessica.

"Tougher than you look," he said.

"I've been around awhile," she replied. "Picked up a few upgrades along the way.

"Likewise," Bes said, and suddenly a lightwand was in his hand.

<*Wow, that was fast,*> Iris said. <*This guy is serious business.*>

<*Thanks, Iris, I hadn't noticed.*>

Bes came at her high with the lightwand, and she ducked to the side, kicking at his leg. He wasn't there when her boot lashed out, instead his own foot slammed into her right knee.

Jessica pivoted just in time to take the blow on the back of the joint, rather than the side, and allowed herself to fall onto her back.

She pulled her knees to her chest, slammed her hands against the deck and straightened into a handstand that sent her feet into Bes's neck and face.

He grunted and fell back as Jessica completed the sinuous maneuver and landed on her feet. She had hoped he would fall and she could deliver a finishing blow, but he still looked ready to go a few more rounds.

By some miracle, however, Bes had dropped the lightwand and it rolled under the table.

Jessica delivered a roundhouse kick to his head, which Bes caught with ease. He smirked and pulled on her leg, but

Jessica was expecting him to do just that. She swung her other leg up at his head while falling back to the floor once more.

She managed to lock her ankles behind Bes's head, and, with every ounce of her strength she launched him over her body and into the bulkhead.

Jessica turned over to get ready for the next round, when a resounding *CRACK* filled the room. She saw Cargo standing over the enemy colonel, one of the room's steel chairs in his hands. Bes was struggling to get up, and Cargo hit him again.

The man finally went down.

"You need to dig deep and find your girl-power, Cargo," Jessica grinned as she gracefully to her feet. "Can't take on one little tin soldier without resorting to furniture."

"More like c-fibre and steel soldier. I think he broke a rib." Cargo gingerly touched his side. "Yup, definitely broke a rib."

Jessica delivered a kick to Bes's head to make sure he was really out before they hauled him to the table and set him beside Admiral Krissy.

<*I can fool scan and their cameras, but once someone actually comes in here, they'll know what's up.*> Iris said.

"Then let's not stick around," Jessica replied.

"Ideas?" Cargo asked. "There's going to be at least two guards in the hall, and they won't be as easy to take down as Bes here.

"Well, you really can't pass as Bes, but I might be able to get past the guards as Krissy…"

"Dream on," Cargo replied. "Your skin is *purple*. Even with her clothes and hair color, those guards aren't going to be fooled for more than a second."

<*I wonder if I* ***could*** *alter the color of your skin,*> Iris mused. <*Or maybe coat it in something close to Krissy's skin color…*>

Jessica looked around the room, which contained only the table, four steel chairs, the rubberized deck, and the four humans.

"Deck's kinda tan," Cargo offered.

<*It's either that, or we wait to see if the hackit you dropped actually makes it here.*> Hank said.

<*I suspect if the hackit were going to take out the guards and get us out of here it would have already,*> Jessica said. <*It must have been picked up, or gotten lost or something—but I really don't like the idea of having melted deck smeared on me.*>

"I'm just going to take a peek out into the hall," Cargo said. "Something tells me that unless we can hack into their network and fool their sensors, nothing we pull off is going to work."

<*Worth a shot,*> Hank said. <*It is surprising that no one came in when you slammed Bes into the bulkhead. That was pretty loud.*>

Cargo walked to the door and waved his hand over the control panel.

To their surprise it opened. Jessica sent a few nanoprobes out into the corridor and saw the guards standing at attention; neither looked toward the open door.

She glanced at Cargo, shrugged, and stepped out into the hall. The guards remained stock still, and she picked up a wireless signal from the hackit.

"The thing made it after all," she said. "It's onboard NSAI has a backdoor into their public network. Good thing this place is a civilian station, or I bet that it wouldn't have managed."

"Or the Transcend doesn't have as much of an edge over you colonists as you'd feared."

"Maybe," Jessica mused. "But it's been almost five-thousand years. How is it that they are still at a level remotely close to 42nd century Sol?"

"The place was a crucible," Cargo offered. "You've told stories about how cutthroat and scheming everyone was."

"True.... Anyway, we've got to find their traffic control center and plant a trigger in the gate control system."

<I've pulled up the station layout,> Iris said. *<You've got a kilometer to go, and I don't think you should hop a maglev—but you better move fast, looks like they're attacking* Sabrina.*>*

"What?" Jessica asked.

<They haven't taken it yet,> Hank added. *<Looks like our people repelled the initial boarding attempts.>*

Jessica nodded with relief while looking at Iris's proposed route to the STC. Then she glanced at the two stock-still soldiers in the corridor.

"I may have an idea."

A LITTLE OUTING

STELLAR DATE: 07.22.8938 (Adjusted Years)
LOCATION: *Sabrina*, Docking Bay F34A, Gisha Station
REGION: DSM Ring, Grey Wolf System

"That was the exact opposite of fun. I've never seen shit used as a weapon quite like that," Cheeky said as she leaned against a bulkhead. "You sure we're clear, Sabs?"

<I sent the repair bots out on the hull, they don't see anything out there.>

"Man…it really stinks down here," Trevor said.

"At least they were nice enough to take their dead and wounded with them," Nance replied. "Corpses in the mix would really take a while to clean up."

"I need to get off this deck before I throw up," Cheeky said, taking slow, shallow breaths as she walked to the ladder.

"Get cleaned up and get in some light armor, Cheeky," Finaeus said. "You and I are going out there."

"Out where?" Cheeky asked.

"There," Finaeus said, gesturing at the hull.

"In environmental?"

"No, stop being dense. Outside the ship."

Cheeky laughed, and in doing so took a deep breath. "Oh stars, oh, I'm going to hurl."

"Don't!" Nance called out from the entrance to environmental. "I've got enough to clean up."

"In related news," Finaeus began, "I think I have an idea about how we can use your ship's stasis shields to mount a film of the material we use for the Ford-Svaiter mirrors. If it will work, then we won't have to mount a physical mirror on the ship. We can deploy it with a grav field, and then support it with the stasis shield."

"Seriously?" Trevor asked as he approached. "Aren't we more worried about getting Jessica and Cargo back and getting out of here? Are you really still this fixated on using the jump gate?"

"If we try to fly through the dark layer, stopping for fuel at predictable jump points, the Grey Division will be all over us like flies on feces."

"Seriously?" Cheeky asked as she reached the top of the ladder. "Didn't you see how I almost tossed my cookies down there?"

Finaeus grinned. "Sorry, it was just front of mind."

<Don't mind me, everyone, I'll just be down here knee deep in shit and algae blooms,> Nance said.

<Sorry, Nance,> Cheeky replied. *<Looks like Finaeus has a very important mission that I need to help on.>*

<And…uh…I need to keep watch over the ship,> Trevor said.

"Really, though," Cheeky said aloud. "Won't we be leaving the ship vulnerable if we go?"

"At this point they're going to try to use Cargo and Jessica as leverage. So, as long as neither of them show up with a gun to their head out there, Trevor can hold down the fort on his own," Finaeus replied.

<I've also deployed all our atmosphere-capable point defense weapons. If they breach again, I'm going to open fire on anyone I can see,> Sabrina said. *<Since you guys already killed a bunch of them, I don't see this ending peacefully anyway.>*

"Good point," Cheeky nodded.

"OK, so where's your armory?" Finaeus asked.

Cheeky led him to the forward weapons lockup, which was hidden behind a panel in one of the cargo bays. Inside lay enough weapons, armor, and gear to start a minor war.

"Seriously, you're pirates," Finaeus said.

"We've only ever attacked and boarded one other ship," Cheeky said. "And *they* were most certainly pirates."

<I think you're forgetting a few other times,> Sabrina said.

"Yeah, but those were all back before we met Tanis and got a letter of marque. In fact, we still have that, we're just operating on behalf of the Silstrand Alliance here."

"Good grief," Finaeus muttered.

"Here," Cheeky gestured to a rack of light, stealth-capable armor sets. "They won't have the tech to fool these folks here, but they should do give us an edge."

<Trevor? what are you doing, Trevor?> Sabrina interrupted.

"Who, me?" Trevor replied, an innocent grin on his face.

<Yes, those are mines you're holding. I can see them.>

"They're little mines, like wee ones, shaped charges, very non-destructive to the ship."

<OK…but be very, very careful. Let's talk about where you plan to put them.>

Cheeky tuned out Trevor and Sabrina's conversation as she stripped out of the clothing Jessica had talked her into wearing and wiped the sweat and grime off her face.

She slid into the armor's base layer which provided additional kinetic energy dispersal and heat management. Then Cheeky backed toward the rack, which wrapped the armor's protective plates around her body, before it attached the helmet.

She saw Finaeus doing the same out of the corner of her eye and smiled as he squirmed uncomfortably as the armor folded itself around him.

Her eyes were covered by the helmet, and her vision went dark for a moment as the gear initialized and fed its optics into her mind via the armor's hard-Link.

<OK, grab one of those rifles, the three-mode ones on the far wall, mags, nades and a sidearm,> Cheeky directed, enjoying being the one who gave the orders on a sortie for once. Usually it was Jessica or Cargo who ran a mission—or Sera back in the day.

<This time I'm going plasma,> Finaeus said.

<Then take another sidearm as well,> Cheeky replied. *<We only have two plasma mags for that model.>*

<What kind of pirates are you?> Finaeus asked with a grin over the Link.

<Har, har, enough already.>

<So sensitive.>

Cheeky grabbed enough mags to shoot her way clear out of Gisha Station, and slipped a flechette pistol and a ballistic pistol into the armor's holsters.

<So what's the plan?> she asked Finaeus once they left the weapons lockup and resealed the panel.

<Best way out is through the maintenance bay down below.>

<Through all the shit and algae and whatever those green slimy tuber things were?> Cheeky asked.

<Well, we need to go around all that. We can't track all that mess everywhere…kinda ruins the whole stealth thing we're trying to achieve. Is there another way out that can get us down into the cradle?>

Cheeky thought about it for a moment. *<Sabrina? Think we can get out through the service hatch down by the D2 fueling ports?>*

<It'll be a tight fit for Finaeus, but I think so,> Sabrina replied after an instant's consideration. *<You'll be right behind one of the cradle struts too.>*

<Nance, hold off on dumping that shit out of the ship, we'll need a distraction.>

<Dump it? Cheeky, this stuff is how we breathe. I need to keep as much of it as possible,> Nance replied with no small amount of chagrin in her voice.

<Well…can you dump some of it?>

<Ok, just a bit, tell me when.>

Cheeky led Finaeus toward the aft end of the cargo level, down a ladder to the engineering deck, and down one more into the service passages that ran under the auxiliary reactor—which was thrumming quietly, but menacingly above them.

They reached the access port and cycled open the inner airlock. Cheeky slipped in and got ready to cycle the outer one. They'd have to leave both doors open at once. She barely fit in the airlock—which was meant for bots, not people—there was no way they both would.

<You ready, Nance? Give me a ten-count before you're going to dump waste.>

<OK, on your HUD.>

Cheeky saw the count and took a deep breath, triggering the outer lock to open at three. Then, when the number hit zero, she leapt down and landed behind a strut and moved over, making room for Finaeus who came down a moment later.

Sixty meters away, she saw a bit of slop, and one of the long tubers fall to the deck.

<That's it? That's your distraction? I thought you'd dump a thousand liters or something.>

<I told you> Nance replied. *<If you want to breath or shower in space ever again, I need this stuff.>*

<Well, now that I see what's really in those tanks, I may never do either again.>

However, by some miracle, none of the Transcend soldiers noticed them. Most were dealing with their wounded, or strengthening their positions now that Sabrina had powered up the point defense systems.

Cheeky looked to Finaeus, who pointed to a narrow space behind one of the cradle's struts where fueling lines rose out of the deck. She could see another level down there, and nodded.

Finaeus sent a pair of microscopic probes down into the lower level and the feed on their HUDs showed only two soldiers.

She prayed to whatever stars were listening that the stealth features on their armor would be enough to hide them. They didn't have full-EM invisibility capabilities, but it should be enough to avoid notice by anything other than an active sensor sweep.

Cheeky slipped through the narrow space around the fuel lines first and looked back up at Finaeus. It would be a tight fit for him, and he passed his rifle down to her before carefully lowering himself down.

The level was filled with tanks, fuel lines, power systems, and the grav emitters that moved the docking cradle's arms. She could see one of the guards walking past a row of SC Batts a few dozen meters away, but the other wasn't visible from her position.

Finaeus led the way toward wherever he thought he could get his special material for the jump gate mirror, while Cheeky kept her eyes peeled—praying she spotted the guard first.

By some miracle, their luck held, and she eventually saw the second guard on the probe's feed, moving away from them, barely paying attention to his surroundings.

They reached a hatch, and Finaeus began to work at the access panel while Cheeky crouched behind some equipment, keeping watch.

She felt the beginnings of butterflies in her stomach—her least favorite part about action like this. Before, when they were on the ship, there had been no time for nerves, and barely enough to see the threat and respond.

But now, away from *Sabrina*, anything could happen. They could be separated from the ship; the ship was safety, it was home. Even when they docked at stations, Cheeky never really strayed far from *Sabrina*. She knew it was foolish, but even after all these years there was still a little fear in the back of her mind that she might get left behind.

Before long, Finaeus completed his work and the panel slid aside, revealing a narrow passageway that appeared to branch out at regular intervals.

Tools and equipment lay on the deck in several places, and Cheeky suspected that when there wasn't a looming battle, workers frequented these lower corridors.

Perhaps Finaeus would find what he was looking for without having to go too far.

<Think he knows where he's going?> Piya asked.

<Who knows…even if he didn't, he'd never say it,> Cheeky replied. *<Super smart, but he strikes me as a serious throwback.>*

<Well, he did grow up in the twenty-fourth century.>

Cheeky shook her head at the thought. Finaeus made Tanis and the *Intrepid* look like recent history. To think that this man left Sol centuries before the first Sentience War was mind-boggling.

And here they were skulking through service corridors like a pair of thieves.

<You kind of are thieves,> Piya said.

<I need to keep my ruminations out of my public mind,> Cheeky said with a laugh. *<Besides, you're a thief too, then.>*

<I'm just along for the ride,> Piya responded innocently. *<If you're caught, I'll say that you kidnapped me.>*

Cheeky saw that Finaeus had stopped ahead, and was looking up and down a cross corridor. He put a hand to his chin, then jerked his head back in surprise. She wondered if he had forgotten that he was wearing a helmet. After a moment he nodded to himself and turned left.

If she hadn't had her HUD showing a map of the path they took, she would have been lost in minutes with all the turns he took. However, it did seem like he wasn't wandering aimlessly. They hadn't backtracked, or crossed their previous route.

They still hadn't run into anyone, and Cheeky was beginning to wonder if they'd walk clear across Gisha and not see a soul, when her armor's advanced sensors picked up voices.

Finaeus seemed blissfully unaware of their impending detection, and she reached out to touch his shoulder. He turned his head back to look at her.

<*What?*> he asked, breaking Link silence.

<*I hear voices ahead.*>

<*Me too, that's why we can't stop. Our destination is just up there.*>

Finaeus began moving again. Cheeky pulled out her sidearm and followed, several drones ahead and behind, watching for movement.

The voices ahead were getting louder and Cheeky was ready to duck behind a tool chest, and engage who ever showed up, when Finaeus stopped at a door, quickly punched in a series of numbers, and ushered her inside as the door opened.

Once inside, Cheeky was surprised to see that they were in some sort of room filed with spare parts…used spare parts. Long racks lined the walls and ran down the length of the room. They were littered with small silver plates haphazardly tossed onto any flat surface, as well as some larger pieces stacked up in corners.

<*This is why security was so light to get here,*> she mused. <*This is the used parts room for jump-gate mirrors, isn't it?*>

<*Hole in one,*> Finaeus replied. <*They guard the new mirrors like the crown jewels, but used and broken bits? Not so much.*>

<*But if they're broken, how are we going to use them on* Sabrina*?*>

Finaeus picked up one of the broken plates from a shelf. <*All I really need is the coating. However, they don't seem to have the tool I need to get it off. I can probably build one back on the ship, but it means we're going to have to grab a lot of these pieces.*>

<*How many?*> Cheeky asked.

Finaeus cocked his head to the side, and held a hand in the air as he worked out the answer. <*Given their distribution…two hundred and seventeen.*>

<*What?*> Cheeky asked. <*How are we going to carry that many back to the ship?*>

<*There's a cart over there,*> Piya suggested with a mental smirk.

<*Right, we'll just wheel that cart half way across the station,*> Cheeky retorted.

<*I was kidding,*> Piya replied.

Finaeus was searching through the shelves, and glanced back at Cheeky. <*This is why I don't have an AI in my head. Their sense of humor is always just a bit off.*>

<*Right,*> Piya said. <*This coming from the guy who thinks everything is a joke.*>

<*Maybe it is,*> Finaeus replied.

<*This isn't helping,*> Cheeky said. <*We can't get the coating off the plates, and we can't haul a cartload of mirror bits through the station, how are we going to get them back to the ship?*>

Finaeus didn't reply as he walked to the far end of the room. Then he gave a laugh. <*Now* ***this*** *is funny. You're gonna love this, Cheeky.*>

HEADACHE

STELLAR DATE: 07.22.8938 (Adjusted Years)
LOCATION: Interrogation Room, Gisha Station
REGION: DSM Ring, Grey Wolf System

Admiral Krissy felt consciousness slowly return. It took a moment to recall what had happened, and then worry flooded her. Those two had better get Finaeus off Gisha safely.

She heard a groan and looked over to see Bes slowly lift his head off the table. Relief came and she resisted sighing. Jessica and Cargo had done it. Taken down Bes and escaped. Now would come the hard part.

He was wearing Cargo's uniform, and she glanced down to see that she was wearing Jessica's outfit. It was really tight on the waist, but the feeling of discomfort was suppressed by the deep-seated joy she felt at seeing Bes in pain. Bes's ever-present scowl deepened and Krissy couldn't help but give a soft laugh.

"I appreciate that look of frustration," she said and Bes glanced at her.

"How long?" Bes asked, still sounding disoriented.

"Just fifteen minutes. Someone should be along shortly."

"How is it that they got the best of you, Admiral?"

Krissy grinned, enjoying Bes being taken down a little too much. "Probably the same way they got the best of you. We underestimated them."

Bes pulled at the shackles that held his wrists to the table. She was about to warn him not to use his nano on the shackles when he jerked in pain.

"Yeah, don't do that," Krissy warned.

"Damnit!" Bes shouted. "Hello! We're in here!"

"Relax," Krissy said. "Someone will be along soon."

Bes shot her an acidic look. "How is it that we've been alone for this long already?"

"Well, I told my people to give me an hour, and it's almost been an hour. They know not to come looking for me unless it's an e—"

The door slid open, almost as though Krissy had willed it, and a lieutenant rushed into the room. "Admiral, the ship—what happened?"

"We were attacked," Bes retorted. "What about the ship? Did you successfully take it?"

"Wait, what? Take the ship?" Krissy asked.

"Yes, Admiral," Bes said, casting a dark look in the woman's direction. "While you were in here chatting up those pirates, I was following my orders."

"How many died?" Krissy asked the lieutenant who was removing her restraints.

"Two," he said quietly. "Seventeen more were critically wounded. The enemy avoided headshots."

"They're not the enemy," Krissy said before delivering her own dark look at Bes. "At least they weren't."

Bes shook his head. "Your attachment to Finaeus is—"

"Only natural," Krissy interrupted. "He was exiled from Huygens, not from the galaxy. He's done nothing wrong—other than the dustup while docking—no matter what your orders say."

"They're your orders too," Bes replied as the lieutenant released his bonds.

"What happened?" Krissy asked the officer.

"Major Michaels attempted to take the ship from two ingress points. He wasn't expecting them to use kinetics within their own ship…or to use their waste treatment systems. They fought us to a standstill, and then allowed us to take our wounded and retreat."

"At least some people still have honor," Krissy said and shot Bes a cold look. "And it's not surprising they used kinetics. They're cornered. Cornered people do desperate things."

Bes walked to the door. "The real question is where are Jessica and Captain Cargo?" He peered out into the hall, noting the absent guards.

"I don't know," the lieutenant replied. "I've raised the silent alarms and posted an alert for the missing guards. They can't move freely around the station, we'll find them."

"Perhaps," Bes replied. "But we've underestimated them before."

He strode into the hall and Krissy followed. He glanced back at her and shook his head. She knew what he was thinking—his orders didn't give him control of the fleets or station. Now that he had tried to go around her and failed, he wouldn't be able to do it again

Krissy thanked her influence with the Admiralty for that. A lot of other commanders would have found themselves at the beck and call of a GD colonel had one arrived at their outpost.

"Admiral, I want you to direct a full-scale attack on the *Sabrina*. We'll take that ship if we have to cut it to ribbons."

"Are you daft?" Krissy asked. "That ship is *inside* our shields, *and* has a stasis shield. They could destroy us if they wished. I suspect only their sense of right and wrong has kept them from escalating things."

"Then what do you propose?" Bes asked. "I would hate to report that you did not discharge your orders to the best of your abilities. And right now, it appears to me as though you are not."

Admiral Krissy walked ahead of him, turning toward the docking bay where the *Sabrina* rested.

"I'm trying to make lemonade out of the lemons you've given me—while *not* killing the former crew of our president's daughter while I'm at it. Or his brother. Or a member of the most powerful group of people in the galaxy. Maybe it's you who is not acting in a fashion that aligns with the Transcend's goals."

Bes didn't respond as he followed her down the corridor, his reticent silence speaking volumes. She was starting to give more and more credit to the idea of a stealthed ship being to blame for the attack on Gisha. Bes appeared to be willing to do whatever it took to secure his prize—as quickly as possible.

She wished for a moment that Finaeus had never come here, that he had found some other jump gate in the Inner Stars.

But then...then he may have been taken already and subjected to who knows what the Grey Division had in mind for him.

A NEW OUTFIT

STELLAR DATE: 07.22.8938 (Adjusted Years)
LOCATION: Command Deck, Gisha Station
REGION: DSM Ring, Grey Wolf System

"I can't believe that they're using this armor," Jessica said. "It's based on a model the Jovian Combine's police forces discontinued in forty-first century. I mean, it's had some upgrades, but still the same software that STR-RV models used back in Sol. It's nuts."

<Makes sense. A lot of software gets layered on top of so much other code that eventually no one even knows how to compile the dependent libraries anymore. Rewriting them could introduce thousands of bugs, so everyone just leaves it all alone,> Iris said.

"Advantageous, though," Cargo said. "Glad you spotted it. I'd rather not have tried walking to their space traffic control center without it. This station is loaded with Sendy Soldiers."

"Let's go with Scenders, can't you here the C? I think it works better"

"Jess, you always get to name everyone. But you got us into this mess, so this time I get to give the bad guys their nickname."

Jessica walked her armor around a corner and spied the entrance to the station's STC a hundred meters down the hall. A pair of guards stood at attention outside the entrance.

"I did not get us into this! You could have said 'no' to Finaeus's crazy plan to come here. You're the captain, after all."

"Not that," Cargo replied. "This whole idea to get captured to get the hackit into their STC."

"You came along, didn't you?" Jessica asked, glancing over at him.

Cargo snorted. "Only because you'd have gotten killed without me. That Bes guy would have mopped the floor with you."

"Hardly!" Jessica barked. "I would have worn him down."

"Sure, sure," Cargo replied. "So, are we going to do this, or what?"

"Yeah, but just use pulse rifles on low. No need to kill any of these folks. Just have to drop the hackit in there."

"On three. One, two, three!"

They kicked the armor into a full speed, charging down the corridor at sixty kilometers per hour toward the station's STC. Expressions of surprise, then terror filled the faces of the guards before they regained some composure and fired their pulse rifles at the onrushing threat. It wasn't enough to slow their attackers down, and the guards dove out of the way at the last minute.

The powered armor made short work of the door, smashing through into a wide room filled with consoles and holotanks. Jessica and Cargo fired at everyone and everything in the STC, creating the biggest distraction they could manage as the hackit dropped from Jessica's armor and rolled under a console where it spread nanofilaments into the system.

"Halt! Stop! What the hell are you doing?" A voice called out over the station's audible address systems, issuing orders which Jessica and Cargo gleefully ignored as they fired concussive pulse shots with wild abandon.

A few holdouts were crouched behind consoles at either end of the STC, and the pair split up, advancing on the final targets. Just as they reached the last pockets of station personnel, automated turrets dropped from the ceiling and opened fire.

The voice over the audible address system called out "You've had your warning!"

Armor-piercing kinetic rounds slammed into the purloined suits and cracked the ablative plating before beams sliced through the underlying layers.

First Jessica's armor ceased moving, followed a moment later by Cargo's.

"Well," Jessica said, sitting up and removing the hard-Link patch that ran from her head to the unconscious soldier next to her. "That's that. We'd better get a move on, they're going to renew their search when they see that those things were on remote pilot."

Cargo nodded as he removed the hard-Link cable from the base of his spine. "Hate using that thing. Makes me feel like a damn robot."

"I bet it felt better for you than him," Jessica said, giving a nod to the unconscious soldier on the ground. "He'll probably have nightmares for a week. I hear remote piloting through someone's Link messes shit up when it comes to body dysphoria."

"Yeah…probably why it's illegal everywhere," Cargo replied.

"I don't even know what legal means anymore," Jessica said as she slid open the door and peered out into the passageway. Across the way was the door to the conference room where they had secured Admiral Krissy and Bes. The door was open, and the room appeared empty. Which meant that the Admiral and Colonel were likely headed to the same place Jessica and Cargo needed to get to: *Sabrina.*

She glanced back down at woman she had jacked into, and the tight, purple shipsuit the soldier wore. It bore a corporal's markings, and would fly under the radar a lot better than Admiral Krissy's uniform.

Not to mention that it matched her hair perfectly.

"I'm going to change," she said to Cargo, "You should too, Bes's uniform will stand out a lot more than that guy's."

"This isn't a fashion show," Cargo grunted. "How many more wardrobe changes you going to make?"

"First off," Jessica said with a grin as she stripped down. "It's *always* a fashion show—you've flown with us women for far too long not to realize that."

"Plus Trevor," Cargo said as he began to undress. "That guy has a wardrobe to match Cheeky's—in volume of clothing, not the amount it covers."

Jessica laughed, and quickly covered her mouth. "Sorry, I just imagined Trevor trying to cover his bits in one of Cheeky's outfits. He's really well—"

"Please!" Cargo whispered. "I get the picture, OK? I sail with the crew of the SS *Fuck*, this isn't news to me."

Jessica chuckled. Cargo really was out of place when it came to that. Even Nance looked positively lascivious next to him. She had to admit that it made the brooding man rather alluring.

"I prefer the SS *Sexy*. Fuck is a bit too on the nose. I wonder if Sabrina would consider that for a name change some time."

"You bring it up and you're on galley duty for a year. I'm not docking anywhere as the captain of the SS *Sexy*—even if it is a ruse for some job."

<Not to mention the incongruity of Jessica claiming that 'Fuck' is too on the nose for her,> Hank said.

Cargo covered his mouth to muffle a laugh, and Jessica couldn't help but smile.

<Any time you want to get back to the mission, that would be great> Iris chided.

Jessica scowled at Iris in her mind, *<Always trying to ruin my fun.>*

<Always? Try practically never.>

Jessica had to admit Iris was right there, and switched to the group's net and addressed the AIs. *<Think you can shroud our faces well enough?>*

<Going to try. There's an alert out for the soldiers you used like sock puppets, so I can't make you look like them. I did piggyback through them into their rosters, so I can pick out a few different people at random. The nanocloud will fool any passive scans, but if they call for a token check, you're screwed.>

<So just like always, then?> Hank asked.

<Good thing their AI are so…weak,> Iris said. *<Makes it easier to outsmart them.>*

<I don't get it at all,> Hank added, as Jessica and Cargo began working their way back toward the ship. *<I mean, I know I'm not too much past an L2, but these AI haven't been shackled for generations. How is it that they're on par with me?>*

<Beats me,> Jessica said. *<Let's just chalk it up to my good luck.>*

Cargo laughed. *<Right, luck.>*

<I have tons of lu—>

Jessica turned the corner to find a temporary security checkpoint set up fifty meters down the corridor.

<Aw, shit.>

Cargo gave short laugh. *<Like I was saying.>*

SPIDER-BOT SAVIOR

STELLAR DATE: 07.22.8938 (Adjusted Years)
LOCATION: Repair & Storage Area, Gisha Station
REGION: DSM Ring, Grey Wolf System

<I don't get it, what is this thing?> Cheeky asked, looking down at the strange, three meter-long robot resting on the deck.

<It's an applicator,> Finaeus said with a broad smile. *<As in it applies the very coating we're looking for to the mirror backing on ships. Probably used for spot repairs where they don't need to replace the entire panel.>*

The thing looked a bit like a spider with engines instead of an abdomen. It must have been an automatic crawler that would move across the surface of a ship's Ford-Svaiter mirror and repair the surface of the mirror.

<Why do these mirrors crack and break so much?> she asked. *<It doesn't really instill confidence.>*

<Well,> Finaeus said as he opened up a panel on the robot. *<This system is a bit of a mess. Dust, rock, grit, it's all out there, and it's all swirling around hard. You can't run a shield in front of your mirror when you jump, so when you drop into a system there's a fraction of a second where the mirror is exposed.>*

<Ahhh…> Cheeky nodded. *<I can see how that would cause some damage.>*

<And guess what?> Finaeus said. *<The bot has a full canister. More than enough to make a mirror for the* Sabrina.*>*

<Fin, you've been with us for weeks, when are you going to learn, it's just 'Sabrina' no 'the'.>

<Right, right, I wonder if that's why she's always so testy with me,> Finaeus muttered absently as he began to loosen the clamps holding the canister of mysterious stuff in place.

<*That, amongst other reasons, I imagine,*> Piya said. <*You're always poking around at her innards.*>

Cheeky decided to check over the rear of the storage area as Finaeus worked. She saw that an airlock lay around a corner at the back of the room. It must be how the service crews got the broken mirror plates in, and where the bot went out—though it was strange that it was here in such a low-security area.

Maybe a repair crew just left it here when the station sector cleared out for *Sabrina*. It would explain why the inner door on the lock was still open.

She walked back around to see Finaeus still fighting with the canister containing the mirror material.

<*Need a hand?*> she asked.

<*No, just…about…got…*> Finaeus grunted each word and then, just when it looked like he had it free, he slipped and fell back.

<*Got it, eh?*> Cheeky chuckled.

She bent over to help Finaeus up, when she heard the door at the entrance slide open, and a voice call out. "You two, check in here. Make sure the airlock's secured."

<*Quick,*> Cheeky hissed. <*Grab it, we'll go out the lock!*>

Finaeus nodded wordlessly and lifted two of the spider-robot's legs while Cheeky grabbed another pair and thanked the stars that the armor augmented her strength. The thing was *heavy*.

They moved as quietly as possible, but Finaeus caught one of the legs on the airlock's door and it made a terrible scraping sound.

Cheeky slammed a fist into the panel to cycle the airlock, but nothing happened.

<*Seriously?*>

<*Hold them off, I'll crack it,*> Finaeus said, as he climbed over the spider-bot to reach the panel. Cheeky crouched behind the

gangly robot, unslung her rifle, and tried to steady her breathing.

She sent a probe out that was almost immediately destroyed by their electronic warfare. However, it did feed a brief image of two soldiers moving down the rows of mirror fragments. She shifted further back into the airlock, doing her best to make sure they couldn't see her before she could fire on them.

Cheeky spotted one soldier's leg through one of the racks. She blew out her breath, took aim, and mentally pulled the trigger on her rifle.

It fired off a three-round burst of kinetic slugs, which slammed into the soldier's shin-plate with a resounding *CRACK*. He danced back, and a beat of pulse blasts hit the airlock's door in response.

<Hurry,> Cheeky urged. *<If they muck up this damn door, the airlock will never cycle.>*

<Hold please…> Finaeus replied.

<What?> Was he cracking jokes?

Another series of blasts hit the airlock's entrance, and Cheeky fired a half-magazine into the racks of mirror parts, hoping to make the enemy fall back.

Instead she heard more boots pounding down the rows.

<Getting to be a lot of company out there!>

<OK…here goes,> Finaeus replied, and a moment later, the inner door sealed, and then the airlock rapid-cycled the outer door, blasting the air, the two humans—and the spider-bot—out into space.

<I don't think this is much better!> Cheeky shrieked as they drifted away from the hub of Gisha Station at an alarming rate.

Somehow, she managed to grasp one of the spider-bot's limbs and then grab onto Finaeus's leg, pulling him close. She swung him toward the bot, and she pulled herself onto its body.

<*Now what?*> Cheeky asked. She glanced over her shoulder, realizing that they were headed straight for the station's outer ring. It would take them some time to reach it, but when they did, it was going to hurt like a bitch.

<*Don't worry,*> Finaeus said. <*This thing is made to fly out to ships. It has these little grav engines on the back. Let me just interface with it. Hold on a sec.... Oh, and get on the bottom, I'll stay on the top. Our armor's stealth systems should make the bot hard to spot.*>

Cheeky carefully worked her way around the bot, holding on with all her might.

Normally she loved space, loved the black, but it wasn't black here. Ships were flying all around them, oblivious to the partially stealthed bot she clung to. Dust pinged off her armor, and above them, the baleful eye of the Grey Wolf Star loomed—its dark band of black holes tearing the star apart, atom by atom.

No, this wasn't the black, this was some sort of space hell, and she was floating around in it with a crazy ancient scientist who may or may not manage to get a stupid spider robot to fly them back to a station where everyone wanted to kill them!

<*Easy now, easy,*> Piya said. <*Deep breaths, the armor has hours of oxygen. You're going to be just fine.*>

<*Easy for you to say!*> Cheeky retorted. <*If I freeze up out here, you can write yourself into static storage and be fine. Me? I'll be a freezer treat. And I didn't even get a good fuck back in Ikoden! I haven't had decent tail in two months! I can't die like this!*>

<*No one's going to die,*> Finaeus said. <*I've done stuff like this dozens of times. We'll be just fine. Look, I have it activated.*>

Sure enough, the spider bot began to move, and a moment later, its grav drive activated, turning it back toward Gisha Station's hub.

<I'll take us to the bay door where Sabrina *is, pass a message through, and then they'll pick us up when they shoot their way out—or whatever they decide to do.>*

Cheeky wanted to berate Finaeus, to ask him how long they were supposed to wait outside the station, but she bit her tongue and tried to calm herself down. He was right, this was under control. One of the crazier things she had ever been involved in, but under control.

Then the spider-bot's grav engine went haywire.

ENOUGH IS ENOUGH

STELLAR DATE: 07.22.8938 (Adjusted Years)
LOCATION: Docking Bay F34A, Gisha Station
REGION: DSM Ring, Grey Wolf System

"What do you mean by, 'they escaped the station'?" Admiral Krissy asked.

"Well," Major Michaels began, "we had cornered them in a service bay, one filled with broken mirror bits. We engaged them, and they got out the airlock."

"Shit!" Colonel Bes swore. "They could be anywhere now, probably headed across the station's surface to their bay."

"Yes, sir, I have crews heading out after them, and patrol craft scouring the station."

"This doesn't make any sense," Krissy shook her head. "Did they get EVA suits somewhere? Did anyone check the emergency locker at that airlock?"

"I'm on it," Major Michaels replied and stepped away to address a pair of lieutenants.

"You don't think they killed themselves by accident?" Bes asked.

"I think that's less likely than *you* killing yourself by accident," Krissy said, earning a dark look from Bes. "No, they wouldn't have died by accident *or* on purpose. They're too smart for that."

Krissy looked up at the ship, its invisible stasis shield continuing to protect it from the soldiers surrounding it.

You'd ***better*** *not be that stupid,* Krissy thought. *Finaeus is going to need you back on that ship if he's to get out of this mess.*

She considered the hack job Jessica—it must have been Jessica, with her TBI training—had performed on the two guards. It was a brilliant move, one that surprised even Krissy.

That armor wasn't supposed to be vulnerable to any attack like that.

She was fast learning that nothing was as it seemed with this crew.

"Then what *are* they playing at?" Bes asked. "If their mission is just to escape, why hit the STC? Why did they come out of their ship in the first place?"

"The first answer is simple," Krissy replied. "They want a mirror. Finaeus must have been certain he could still get one, even after they had their misfiring."

"You mean where they attacked the station," Bes said. Krissy noted by his inflection that he meant it as a correction, not a question.

"Oh, is that what happened?" Krissy asked, peering in to the Grey man's eyes, curious if he would let a tell slip through his cold expression.

None did.

"You saw the logs—from your own ships. They don't lie. Not all of them," Bes said while holding her gaze.

Krissy nodded slowly. Until a few hours ago she would have believed that without reservation. Now…not so much.

"No luck so far, Admiral," Major Michaels said as he turned back to them. "I'd like to take another crack at that ship. We're certain we have a plan that will work this time."

"No," Krissy said with a wave of her hand. "You've already squandered what chance we had of winning this without further bloodshed. First, we try to find their compatriots, then we try to negotiate. If that fails, then you go in."

"Yes, ma'am," Major Michaels nodded.

"Major, I'd like to hear your plan," Bes said.

"Belay that, Major!" Krissy turned to Bes, a fire rising in her chest. "*Colonel* Bes. May I remind you that I have orders to capture and turn over two people from that ship, and arrest the rest. Nowhere in my orders does it even *insinuate* that I have to give you one iota of tactical control over this situation. So, if you'll kindly shut up and return to your ship, I'll consider not filing charges of insubordination. *Consider* not—you better have good protection from the top."

Major Michaels blanched, and Bes opened his mouth to deliver a rejoinder when Krissy held up a finger. "I'll remind you, Bes, that we are deep in the Inner Stars, and are on a war footing. Out here, in this realm, I am your god. The Grey Division may be safely back on Airtha, beyond my reach, but you, Bes, you are within my grasp. You'd do well to remember that."

"Admiral," Bes ground out. "The Division will hear of this."

Krissy felt her calm slipping away entirely. "One more word and we'll see if they can hear it from my brig. *Now get out of my sight!*"

To his credit, Bes spun on his heel and left the bay without another word, and Krissy turned her eyes to Major Michaels. She took a slow breath as the man visibly wilted before her.

"Major. The next time someone shows up here—and I don't care who it is, it could be President Fucking Tomlinson—you don't surrender tactical control of an operation without first clearing it with me. Am I clear?"

"Yes, Admiral Krissy."

"Am I *crystal* clear?"

"Yes, Admiral Krissy!"

"Good! Now go do your fucking job—somewhere out of earshot would be nice."

Krissy felt shame over losing her temper so spectacularly—especially while in hearing range of hundreds of her soldiers. Still, it didn't hurt for them to be reminded that the admiral had teeth and she wasn't afraid to use them.

She looked back up at the *Sabrina* wondering if Finaeus was looking down at her. Someone was playing a dangerous game, and she wondered who it was. One thing was for certain, some of his crazier ramblings were starting to make sense.

Krissy turned and surveyed the troops in the bay. Her faith in Major Michaels and his operation was only a hair above nil right now.

<Major Nelson,> she called the *Regent Mary*'s XO. *<Get Lin on the bridge and coordinate a sweep of the exterior of the station. Two of the* Sabrina*'s crew got outside and I need someone I can trust to find them.>*

<You'd be surprised to know that Lin is actually up here, but I'll make sure it gets done,> Nelson replied.

<Good. Nelson, your service will be rewarded. We just need to get through this.>

<Yes, Admiral. Thank you, Admiral.>

Krissy closed the connection and her gaze settled on a pair of soldiers moving toward the ship. There was something familiar about them.

A WINK AND A NOD

STELLAR DATE: 07.22.8938 (Adjusted Years)
LOCATION: Docking Bay F34A, Gisha Station
REGION: DSM Ring, Grey Wolf System

"I say we just walk on," Jessica suggested.

"What? Past all those Sender soldiers?"

"Are you just messing with me now? You gotta say the *C*."

<*I think we could call them Scenties,*> Iris offered.

"I like that," Cargo chuckled. "Scenties."

Jessica put a hand to her forehead and shook her head slowly, turning her attention back to the scene before the pair of them. They stood on one of the upper catwalks in Docking Bay F34A, *Sabrina* lying below them and the growing contingent of TSF soldiers arrayed around it.

"Doesn't seem like she took any damage," Jessica said. "With any luck we can use the hackit to get the doors open and get the heck out of here."

<*We didn't get the mirror, though,*> Hank said. <*I thought that was the whole plan.*>

"Yeah, back before we realized that Krissy is being forced to take orders from the dark side and is going to ship us all off to some secret prison or something."

"Probably the secret prison for me, and the 'or something' for you," Cargo grinned. "Anyway, I like your plan. We just walk toward the ship, maybe cut across the front down there so that it's not obvious until the last moment, and then we run."

"Think Sabrina will spot us and have a lock open?" Jessica asked.

<*I'll tightbeam her,*> Hank said <*She'll have a lock open. Looks like there was a fight at the port one, so let's do starboard—just in case something's messed up.*>

"Fine by me," Jessica replied.

The pair walked to a lift and rode it down to the dock's main level where they casually strode past a platoon setting up a pair of crew-served slug throwers and another group of soldiers readying armor-piercing javelin missile launchers.

<*Some serious ordnance,*> Iris commented. <*If we didn't have stasis shields I'd be concerned.*>

<*What? Traipsing in front of the people who want to kill us in just these shipsuits and a nanocloud to shroud us isn't enough to worry you?*> Jessica asked.

<*Nah, you look too good doing it,*> Iris said with a mental grin.

<*Well, of course I do.*>

They passed by a pair of scouts who were crouched behind a stack of crates, their railguns trained on the starboard airlock.

Jessica was about to suggest that maybe the approach was too dicey when the sound of yelling caught her attention. She glanced over her shoulder and saw Admiral Krissy dressing down a major who looked absolutely terrified.

<*She and Tanis would get on famously,*> Iris said.

<*Or they'd try to kill each other,*> Jessica replied.

Jessica's gaze lingered a moment too long and she cringed as Krissy looked their way and caught Jessica's eye. The admiral frowned.

<*Aaannd the jig is up,*> Hank sighed.

They kept moving hoping against hope that the next words weren't, 'seize them!'.

To Jessica's relief, Admiral Krissy called out to the two scouts watching the starboard lock, repositioning them further down the dock, creating an opening for the pair.

Jessica touched Cargo's shoulder. <*Let's go, now.*>

Cargo didn't respond, but cut across the remainder of the TSF soldiers' front line, then took a deep breath and walked out into the no-man's land around the ship.

For a moment, Jessica thought that they'd pass through free and clear, but then a voice called out.

"Hey! What are you doing?"

"Stop!" another voice hollered.

Jessica broke into a run, dodging and weaving just in case anyone decided to shoot. She saw Cargo doing the same out of the corner of her eye and nearly stumbled when a shot did ring out, and a projectile whistled past her ear.

She poured on as much speed as she could. Hopefully Sabrina did see them and would make a hole, or she was going to slam at full speed into the stasis shield. She was wondering if she'd passed beyond its protection yet when a pulse blast hit her in the back and sent her sprawling.

The staccato beat of projectiles ricocheting around her brought her back to her feet, expecting to see rounds tearing through her.

But she was unharmed.

Jessica turned and saw bullets, rail pellets, and beamfire all striking an invisible force mere centimeters from her face.

She was through the stasis shield.

"You don't see that every day," Cargo said.

<Gonna get in already, or just enjoy the view of not dying?> Sarina asked.

<Stars, it's good to hear your voice,> Cargo replied as the pair ran to the starboard airlock. There was no gantry, and they clambered up and rolled onto the deck floor as the lock cycled.

<Get it warmed up,> Cargo ordered. *<We're getting the hell out of here.>*

<You may want to hold off on that,> Nance said. *<Cheeky and Finaeus aren't aboard.>*

<What!> Jessica exclaimed, struggling to her feet as the inner lock door opened.

<They left to get some material to make a mirror for the ship,> Nance replied. *<That was almost an hour ago, though.>*

<Nothing was on the nets about them being captured,> Iris said. *<Though I disconnected when we were in the bay. Let me see if I can still hook up.>*

As they talked, Jessica and Cargo ran down the starboard passage, climbed the ladder to the crew deck, and then the next up to the command deck.

They entered the bridge to see Nance sitting at one of the scan consoles.

"What do you mean they left?" Cargo growled. "Whose dumb idea was that, anyway?"

"I'll give you three guesses," Nance said quietly.

<My tap's still good,> Iris said. *<Stars…these guys need to improve their security. I bet someone figured infiltration of Gisha would never happen, and got lazy.>*

"I'd rather they left it as weak as possible," Cargo said. "What's the word."

<Weird…there's some sort of search going on out there,> Iris said. *<Oh! They think it's us—well, they did till they saw us on the dock just now.>*

"Out where?" Cargo asked brusquely.

<Sorry, yes, outside the station,> Iris said.

"What?" Jessica yelled.

"Jess! Damn I'm glad you're OK," Trevor said as he burst onto the bridge. "I take it you're yelling about Cheeky and Fin going on a little walkabout."

"Yeah, they walked right off the station."

"What…you're kidding, right?"

"It seems not," Cargo said. "Options, people. They're out there looking for our crew, and we need to reach them first, then get the hell out of here."

<Krissy has mobilized her fleet to search for them, so have the station S&R crews. So far no one has seen hide nor hair of them.>

Jessica threw an image of Gisha on the main holo, and Iris populated it with the last known location of Finaeus and Cheeky.

"Any chance that they faked the Teebies out and are still in the station?" Cargo asked.

"Really? Teebies?"

"Seems like a stretch," Nance shook her head.

<*Hard to say,*> Iris interjected, sounding annoyed at the banter. <*But they're scouring this part of the station with everything they have. If those two are still onboard, they're as good as caught. It'll be a lot better if they're in space.*>

<*They took the XR-79 armor we picked up in Virginis,*> Sabrina said.

"So, two to three hours tops before they run out of air," Cargo said. "Depending on how much Cheeks is hyperventilating right now."

Jessica could only think of one way to get off Gisha, and that was opening fire on the soldiers and the bay doors. But after what Krissy had done to help….

"Only way out of this tin can is to shoot our way out," Cargo said, echoing her thoughts. Jessica met his eyes and the captain sighed. "Right, but we have to warn Krissy somehow."

"What? The evil admiral who is trying to take us all out?" Nance asked.

"It's more complicated than that. She has some significant history with Finaeus—more than just a few drinks once, like he said—enough for her to help us escape. I don't think she wants to see him die."

"Yeah, but he's not here anymore," Trevor said. "She has no special attachment to us."

<*She needs us,*> Iris said. <*If she picks up Finaeus, she has to turn him over to Bes. But if we can pick up the old man, we can jet off with him.*>

<That may be tricky…depending on how much they shoot at us,> Sabrina said.

"Why's that?" Cargo asked.

<Well, SC Batt 3 blew a cooling loop, and it's out. We've been running on our secondary reactor—which is why it's a few degrees warmer in here than normal. We're venting heat out various places as I flicker the stasis shields…>

Cargo let out a long breath. "But once we get out into space…we have to bubble the whole ship."

"Right. No heat dispersion," Nance added.

"Batts one and two look good," Cargo noted.

<Stasis shields suck up the batts pretty fast, especially when they're shedding beams from five-hundred enemy ships,> Sabrina said.

"OK, so it's going to be dicey out there," Jessica said. "But we still—"

<Message from the admiral,> Sabrina said. *<Should I put it on the tank?>*

"Yeah, but just show her Jess and me. Leave her guessing about who else is still onboard."

Admiral Krissy appeared on the holotank, her surroundings a blank grey—which told Jessica that the message was coming from her mind and not visible to anyone near her.

"Captain Cargo, Jessica," she said. "Please ensure that this message is encrypted properly per TSF Naval code 837.322.11A."

Admiral Krissy began to recite the charges against them and the crimes and punishments they faced in a droning, monotone.

Jessica glanced at Cargo and mouthed 'what?'.

<Oh! I know!> Iris exclaimed. *<Yup! She hid an encryption key in one of their databases on rules and regs. Pulling it out…here you go, Sabrina.>*

<*Got it,*> Sabrina replied. <*Aha! A subchannel in the transmission, audio only, putting it through.*>

Suddenly Admiral Krissy's voice changed—though the visual did not.

"Good, I hoped you'd figure that out."

"What's going on, really," Jessica asked pointedly. "What does Finaeus mean to you?"

The admiral didn't reply for a moment, though her image kept moving, soundlessly reciting the charges they faced.

"Ah, what the hell," Krissy finally said. "He's my father."

<*Pay up!*> Iris demanded.

<*Fine,*> Sabrina said.

Jessica wondered what currency the AI were exchanging as a result of their bet—and why she hadn't been in on it. Aloud she said, "That explains a lot."

"He's the one that's out there, isn't he?" Krissy asked. "Just like him to go on some hair-brained adventure. Station can't find him, but my fleet's sensors picked up a ping out past the docking ring. Could be nothing, or it could be them. A man I can trust on my flagship has suppressed it from the logs, but as you know, I can't rescue them. I'll be damned if I'm going to turn my own father—one of the founders of the Transcend—over to the Greys to do whatever it is they do."

Her voice paused and Cargo looked to Jessica, his face showing more emotion than she expected. She wondered what was troubling him.

"You have to get him, and get out of here," Admiral Krissy finally said.

"How will we get out of the docking bay?" Jessica asked. "Without killing all your people, that is."

"If you fire up your main reactor and warm up your engines…slowly, I'll pull everyone back and get someone to trigger an emergency release on the cradle and bay doors. Lloyd would probably do it. He's been having kittens ever since you docked—though he might have upgraded to elephants when you shot up the STC."

"OK, deal," Cargo said.

<I have the coordinates of that ping,> Sabrina said. *<It's a ways out, almost twenty-thousand-klicks.>*

"You need to hurry," Krissy said. "If they get too much further, they'll pass out of the gravitational doldrums…."

She didn't have to finish her statement. Everyone knew that beyond the doldrums lay the crosscutting gravitational fields of the black holes and the Grey Wolf Star.

<Powering up the main reactor,> Sabrina said without waiting for an order from Cargo.

"Good, you'll—shit! Lieutenant, raise the *Excelsia* now! I want that ship to stand down!"

"What is it?" Jessica asked.

"It's Bes, he's coming around with his destroyer and they're powering weapons."

"Stasis shield to max!" Cargo yelled. "Widen it to protect Krissy's people!"

Jessica dropped into the pilot's seat. If Bes wanted a fight, they'd give him a fight. He'd find out that this little freighter had some sting in her.

"Trevor! Weapons!" Cargo called out as he took the command seat. "Power all beams, get the RMs in the tubes."

"Yes, Captain," Trevor replied.

Jessica brought up the bay doors on her holodisplay, praying for the cradle to release its clamps before Bes fired on them.

"Come oooooon," she whispered, then let out a cheer as a light flashed on her console, indicating that the cradle was opening up.

And then the bay's exterior doors exploded.

Laser and particle beam fire tore into the space, splashing off Sabrina's stasis shields, and melting the walls around the ship.

<*They're clear! Krissy cleared the bay. Go!*> Sabrina cried out.

Jessica activated the port and starboard grav drives, directing their graviton wash along the half-melted bulkheads, trying not to shred too much of the station behind them as they pushed out against the withering fire from Bes's ship—which floated a scant two kilometers beyond Gisha's hub.

"I can't believe he's doing this!" Nance cried out. "He's attacking his own people."

"I'm really getting why Sera wanted Finaeus back in play," Cargo said. "Transcend is really not some happy unified utopia."

"Keep it up, asshole," Jessica said through gritted teeth as *Sabrina* cleared the station and she fired their dorsal boosters—slowly, so that Bes would keep his weapons fire on them and not tear a hole right through Gisha Station.

"Fire proton beams on that ship the moment we're clear of the station," Cargo ordered.

"All clear!" Jessica called out a moment later.

"Eat this, asshole!" Trevor yelled as *Sabrina's* four proton beams, courtesy of the *Intrepid's* engineers, blasted protium at the *Excelsia*.

Bes was firing too much, too fast, which meant his shields were open to let his own continuous stream of weapons fire out. Not all the time, but enough for *Sabrina's* proton beams to get through.

Unfortunately, it also meant that when Trevor cracked the shields for *Sabrina*'s weapons to shit, the enemy's beams got in as well.

<*We just lost forty centimeters of our bow plating!*> Sabrina cried out.

"Shit!" Trevor said. "He's throwing everything he has at us. We can't pick up Cheeky and Fin like this!"

"We'll give him the AP nozzle," Cargo said. "Trevor, time the beams with it, and when he's blind, kick out a pair of limpets."

"Spinning out the nozzle," Jessica responded.

The antimatter pion drive's nozzle was a hard target to hit. It only protruded a centimeter beyond the shields, and was just a few centimeters across. However, it emitted a concentrated stream of gamma rays. Combined with the beams, it would do some serious damage to the *Excelsia,* and hopefully take out the vessel's forward shields allowing the limpet mines to attach.

Hopefully.

"Any activity from the station or Krissy's fleet?" Cargo asked.

"Station took damage to fire control systems when Bes shot them up," Krissy said. "And I'm delaying things with my fleet, you have maybe three minutes."

"Shit! Didn't realize you were still with us," Cargo replied.

"Gotta go now, keeping this channel open any longer will look suspicious. Oh, thanks for saving my people and my ass in here."

"No problem," Cargo replied.

<She's gone now,> Sabrina said. *<Sorry about that, with all the excitement I forgot to mention that she was still here.>*

"Ready to boost," Jessica announced. "Going to fire attitudes and line up in three, two, one!"

Though she gave the count aloud, she also passed it to Trevor over the link. Once the gamma rays lanced out and hammered the *Excelia*'s shields, Trevor fired the dorsal proton beams, and the x-ray lasers.

Bes's ship returned fire and an explosion shook *Sabrina.*

<Port dorsal proton beam is gone,> Sabrina reported.

"But so are their forward shields," Nance called out. "Bet you didn't think we had bite like that, suckas!"

"Fuck yeah!" Trevor added.

Jessica smiled, but kept her focus on her boost. The AP drive was still running, and she was jinking side-to-side, making them a hard target to hit as they flew past Gisha's outer docking ring and looped behind one of the heavy-matter haulers.

"Nance, any pings from our wanderers?" Cargo asked? "We need to find them before Jessica has to kill the drive."

"I've been working with the girls. We have it narrowed down to a cone that's about a half-million square klicks," Cheeky said.

Jessica coughed. "Shit, Nance, I'm going to need something more precise than that."

"Head down the probability curve I drew out," Nance replied.

Jessica brought up the data on her console and saw the path she needed to follow.

"Are you kidding me? That has me boosting straight at one of the black holes!"

<*Exhilarating, isn't it?*> Erin asked.

"When did you become such a thrill-seeker?" Jessica retorted as she adjusted the ship's vector down the center of the cone."

"*Excelsia* is coming about," Trevor replied. "I think one of the limpet's attached, not sure about the other."

"Fucker's gonna have a bad day," Cargo said.

"One of us is," Jessica muttered as *Sabrina* continued to pick up speed. On the forward holo, the Grey Wolf Star and its dark ring housing the forty spinning black holes grew in size.

THE NOT SO BLACK HOLE

STELLAR DATE: 07.22.8938 (Adjusted Years)
LOCATION: Between Gisha Station and the DSM Ring
REGION: DSM Ring, Grey Wolf System

<I just want you to know that this is the worst plan ever,> Cheeky said, barely keeping her mental tone from wavering.

<I'll admit that I've had better,> Finaeus replied. *<It's really a shit choice. Send out a signal and get picked up by Bes's goons, or fall into a black hole.>*

<Won't we just hit the ring?> Cheeky asked as she shifted her grip on the bottom of the spider-bot. At least Finaeus had managed to kill its grav drives. Of course, now he couldn't get them working again.

By her calculations, they were about five-thousand klicks from the edge of the doldrums. Once they passed out of the calm space around Gisha Station, punishing gravitational waves would sweep over them—probably killing them long before they reached the ring anyway.

<Nah, it's doubtful,> Finaeus replied. *<The waves will sweep us up over the ring. We'll probably fall into the star. Though, to be honest, it's a bit hard to calculate off my visual observations.>*

<You seem rather chipper about this,> Cheeky groused.

<I've lived a long life,> Finaeus replied. *<I came to accept long ago that the universe will carry on just fine without me.>*

<Speak for yourself,> Piya exclaimed.

<Well I haven't! I'm only fifty-five—lots of living left in me!> Cheeky added.

<I'm coming around to your side,> Finaeus said. *<Once I get over there, use your armor's attitude jets to put the other side of the bot between us and the star. It's gonna get hot, and we're gonna have to hold on for dear life.>*

<'Kay,> was all Cheeky managed to get out.

She knew she was supposed to be tougher. Hard as steel like Sera and Tanis, but she just couldn't do it. Fear kept tearing at the edges of her sanity and she shifted nervously as Finaeus climbed over the bot, setting it spinning.

He wrapped his arms around the bot's legs and hooked a leg around her as well.

<*You'll get a better grip this way,*> he said.

Cheeky didn't reply as she steadied her trembling limbs and managed to get her arms and back in the right positions. She cross checked her thrust estimates with Piya, and fired the jets, and slowing their spin, and then finally stabilizing them.

Then she carefully resumed her prior position, her back to the bot—and the terrible sight beyond it—instead staring up at Gisha Station, praying that someone up there would rescue them, but terrified if she sent a signal it would be the wrong someones.

<*Really, you should turn around. You need a better grip on the bot,*> Finaeus said softly.

Cheeky bit her lip and shook her head, but did hook an elbow around one of the bot's limbs. Then Finaeus moved closer, wrapping an arm around her and laying a leg over hers.

<*I've got you, Cheeky. We're going to make it. Trust me.*>

Cheeky didn't know why he bothered. They were going to die. He knew it. She knew it. There was no point in sugar-coating the truth.

She wished she could close her eyes, but her armor fed a continuous view into her mind, highlighting the safety of Gisha Station that was so far beyond their reach.

Ships swarmed around the station, likely searching for them—though none had ventured beyond the outer docking ring. There was little chance any would reach the pair clinging to the bot, even if they did send out a signal.

Then an explosion flared on the side of the station's central hub, and she saw beamfire lance out and hit one of the ships.

She cycled her vision and saw the familiar shape of *Sabrina* emerge from the station, its stasis shields flaring brighter than the grey star's light as it took blow after blow from one of the Transcend ships.

<*Finaeus!*> she cried out. <*It's* Sabrina*!*>

<*I see them,*> Finaeus replied. <*Don't signal them yet, we need them to get closer.*>

<*How would they know to get closer?*> Piya asked. <*They won't have a clue where we are.*>

<*I sent a ping—one Krissy will know came from me. She'll tell them to get us.*> Finaeus replied.

<*Krissy? The bitch who wants to kill us?*> Cheeky exclaimed. <*Have you lost your mind?*>

Finaeus gave a rueful chuckle in response. <*Maybe, but do you see any TSF ships heading for us?*>

Cheeky didn't, and wondered how Finaeus could have been so sure. Still, none of the TSF ships were moving toward their position, so maybe Finaeus did have some sort of special bond with Krissy.

She watched as *Sabrina* shot back at their attacker, then fired its engines, cutting into the enemy ship in a brilliant display of energy.

Cheeky was about to signal *Sabrina* when she suddenly felt very heavy and her back slammed hard into the bot. The armor took the brunt of the blow, but she was unable to breathe—her diaphragm couldn't move enough to draw air into her lungs.

<*Fin…*>

<*Hold, just a minute longer,*> Finaeus replied.

In a breath the weight was gone, but then, just as suddenly it pushed the other way, and she clung desperately to the bot's limbs.

<Fin! Help!>

A strong arm wrapped around her, and Cheeky was glad for the augmented strength the armor gave them as they were pushed and pulled, slammed into the spider bot, and then pulled away, shearing forces tearing through their bodies.

<Hold on Cheeky. Hold on just a little longer, they'll be here!>

Then a crushing gravity wave washed over Cheeky. The limb of the spider-bot that she was clinging to tore free and she spun away into space.

<Fin!> she called out

<Signal now!> Fin called back. *<Beacon on max!>*

Piya beat her to it, and the armor sent out its beacon, a tiny radio spec in the blinding noise surrounding the Grey Wolf Star and the black holes that raced around it, tearing it apart, atom by atom.

Cheeky began to hyperventilate, and thought she might pass out from the fear, pain, and increasing heat, when Piya stepped in and forcibly regulated her breathing.

<Easy love, easy, take it easy,> the AI whispered in her mind, trying to calm her.

<I don't want to die!> Cheeky cried out in response. *<Piya, I can't…I don't know what to do!>*

Panic tore its way into her mind and she spun about, searching for something to grab on to. She couldn't see Finaeus and the spider-bot anywhere and began to sob into her helmet's breathing apparatus, her throat starting to blister from the stifling air she was drawing in.

A detached part of her mind noted that just as Finaeus had predicted, she began to drift above the ring. The light of the Grey Wolf Star growing brighter as the ring occluded less of it.

More and more heavy gravitational waves slammed into her and she began to periodically lose consciousness as her body fluctuated between weightlessness and dozens of *g*'s. She knew that if it hadn't been for the rigidity of the armor, death would have come long ago.

Cheeky began to feel calm, surprised at the change in her mental state...she would have expected the panic to worsen, but as she crossed over the edge of the ring all she could do was marvel at the beauty of what lay before her.

<*It's not peace or acceptance. Your brain is hemorrhaging,*> Piya said. <*My power hookups are screwed...shit...we're both dying, Cheeky.*>

<*I didn't think they'd be so bright,*> Cheeky replied as she saw the black holes racing around the inside of the ring, glowing with beautiful colors as they consumed small clouds of atoms smeared around their event horizon.

<*Cheeky, stay focused!*> Piya yelled into her mind. <*I'm trying to repair, to keep us going, but I need you conscious.*>

<*I will,*> Cheeky mumbled. <*It's getting so hot...are my hands glowing...but I want to see the lights before I go...*>

RACE AGAINST GRAVITY

STELLAR DATE: 07.22.8938 (Adjusted Years)
LOCATION: Sabrina, between Gisha Station and the DSM Ring
REGION: DSM Ring, Grey Wolf System

"I got a signal!" Nance cried out. "Passing it over, Jess. It's just on this side of the mining ring."

"Got it, adjusting…shit they're moving fast."

<*It split!*> Sabrina called out. <*There's two signals now.*>

"I'm going to have to brake hard and then swoop down. Someone get in a suit and get down to the bay," Jessica replied.

"I have it," Cargo said as he raced off the bridge.

Jessica clenched her teeth as she spun the ship and fired the AP drive at max burn, careful not to send the gamma rays anywhere near the two signals that they were trying to reach.

Sabrina passed out of the doldrums and began to buck and heave as the gravitational waves washed over them.

"Are the dampeners broken?" Trevor asked as he frantically adjusted his seat's straps so he could buckle in.

<*No,*> Sabrina replied. <*Running them on minimum to conserve energy. We've completely drained one of our SC Batts, and the* Excelsia *is hitting us again with their beams. Need to conserve power.*>

Jessica realized that the temperature in the bridge had been increasing and that her brow was slick with sweat.

<*The shipsuit you're wearing has cooling systems,*> Iris suggested.

<*Shoot, thanks,*> Jessica replied as she activated it, keenly aware that Trevor and Nance were going to have to sweat it out as the ship began to grow warmer.

<*I've almost matched* v,> she called down to Cargo.

<Just about done suiting up. It's over forty-fucking-degrees down here. Sweating my balls off.>

<You have seventy seconds to get the bay open, or we're gonna lose the second signal!> she hollered across the Link.

<'Kay, 'kay!> Cargo shouted back.

Jessica knew not to pester him further, but she couldn't stop biting her lip as the ship shook and rattled around them. If they were taking this much abuse *in* the ship, what were Cheeky and Finaeus going through out in the black.

<Bay's open, kick us over. I'm anchored and will catch,> Cargo called up.

<On it,> Jessica replied, and fired the port thrusters, shoving the ship over, and slowing it with the starboard engine just as they came down onto the first signal.

She held her breath and a rivulet of sweat ran into her eye. She swiped it way with an angry gesture. *<Did you—?>* she asked.

<Yeah, secure. It's Finaeus. He's a mess, but alive. Go get Cheeky.>

<On it!> Jessica replied before shouting, "Shit! Where is she?"

"She slipped over the rim," Nance gasped.

"Gonna slingshot around," Jessica said. *<Cargo, she's going to come in hot!>*

Metaphorically and physically.

Jessica spun the ship and fired the drives, heading high over rim of the ring, *Sabrina* describing a tight parabola as it peaked and came back down—straight toward one of the black holes that was racing past.

"Nance! I need a lock, *NOW!*"

"Fuck, Jess…so much noise, we can't pick up anything!"

Iris highlighted the most likely path Cheeky would have taken, and Jessica aimed the ship as best she could as the waves of gravity and stellar matter threw the vessel about.

Her readout showed that it was over fifty-six-degrees on the bridge. She didn't even want to look at the temperature in the cargo bay, but her eye still darted to the panel above the main holo and saw that it was four-hundred-degrees.

"*C'mon*…I need a lock!" she shrieked.

"There! There! There!" Nance yelled back and Sabrina passed the coordinates to Jessica. She altered course and spun the ship once more, aiming the cargo bay door at the infinitesimal spec in the distance.

<*Shit's starting to glow in here!*> Cargo called up. <*Hurry already!*>

<*Nance! I need you in the forward shield emitter room, now,*> Finaeus's weak voice called out over the shipnet.

<*Finaeus, are you OK? Why should I go there?*>

<*Because if you don't, we're gonna die in this system. I can get us out of here, but I need your help.*>

Jessica looked back to Nance. <*Go. The girls can handle scan. Maybe Finaeus has an ace up his sleeve.*>

<*Could sure use one,*> Trevor said as he directed beamfire back at the *Excelsia* which had followed beyond the stellar ring.

Jessica turned her attention back to the drifting form of Cheeky as another gravitational wave from the black holes washed over the ship, pushing it off course once more.

She found herself working faster and faster, leveraging computational power from Iris, until at the last moment, she fired the lateral thrusters and waited for Cargo's confirmation.

One…two…three, she counted in her mind, trying not to scream from anticipation. Either Cheeky was safely in the cargo bay, or she had burned up in the port engine.

<*Got her!*> Cargo called up. <*Fuck, she's hot. Getting her up to the medbay. Get us out of here!*>

<*There's still Bes's destroyer out there,*> Sabrina said. <*I can't keep running our stasis shields and powering drive containment.*>

Jessica swore softly. It sure would be nice if Krissy could extend her help to taking out that asshole.

<Triggering the mines,> Trevor announced. *<I hope they attached.>*

Jessica glanced at the main holo tank and saw two explosions register on scan.

<Looks like you had a good latch,> Jessica sighed with relief. *But was it enough?* she thought to herself.

<Nance. Trevor. Suit up. I want to blow our atmosphere and pump our compressed nitrogen into the ship. My delicate bits are starting to take damage.>

Jessica barely heard Sabrina as relief over Cheeky's rescue and the mines taking out Bes's ship flooded her mind—but just for a second. She still had to dance around the black hole ahead of them.

For a moment, she stopped to marvel at the beauty of the thing, darkness wrapped in light as it fed on matter, held in place by powerful magnetic rails. It was only a kilometer across, but the energy it spewed out of its jets as it consumed the bits of star that entered its event horizon were breathtakingly beautiful.

<Brace!> she called out, as she spun the ship and accelerated toward the black hole, building speed, aiming for a tight slingshot and breakaway back around the ring, to safety—she hoped.

Sabrina began to buck and shimmy even more, and a panel fell off the overhead and smashed into the deck beside her, before another jolt sent it toward the weapons console. She saw it smash into the console's chair and was glad to see Trevor wasn't there—thank the stars Sabrina had directed them to get into suits.

<Got it!> Trevor called out, and she saw him in an emergency EVA suit, wrestling the dislodged panel into a safety net.

<*Cutting it close,*> Sabrina warned Jessica, <*A degree off, you're off…*>

<*Shut it!*> Jessica snapped. She knew what she was doing, if they played it safe, they would never achieve breakaway velocity.

Suddenly Trevor slammed a helmet over her head, and Jessica winced as it clamped around her neck. She had totally forgotten that she wasn't wearing a helmet and would have died when Sabrina vented the atmosphere—though hopefully the ship's AI would have reminded her first.

Proximity alarms blared on the bridge, but then fell silent as the atmosphere rushed out of the vessel. At the exact same moment, Jessica fired both fusion engines on full burn, dumping two-hundred percent the recommended volume of Deuterium and Helium 3 into the reactors.

The ring and flaring black hole flashed past—less than five hundred meters off *Sabrina*'s bow—and then they were past the worst of the gravitational waves, clear dark space ahead of them.

Jessica turned to watch the holotank, praying that Bes's ship didn't emerge from behind the ring. Scan was a mess and they weren't sure if the limpet mines had destroyed the *Excelsia*. If that ship emerged from behind the ring, she didn't know that they would be able to defend against it.

Then an explosion flared at the edge of the ring, and Jessica let out a long breath and slumped into her seat. They'd done it. They were safe.

<*Faawk!*> Trevor exclaimed. <*Let's never do that again, 'kay?*>

Jessica didn't respond, her entire body shaking from the adrenaline coursing through her veins.

<*Easy now, deep breaths. That was some brilliant maneuvering you pulled there at the end, I was certain you were going to smash us into the ring,*> Iris said.

<*Yeahhhhh,*> Jessica managed to utter before scan updated and she saw the ships approaching them. <*Ah shit…*>

<*Looks like their entire fleet,*> Sabrina said. <*Krissy is hailing us.*>

<*Ignore it for a minute,*> Jessica said. <*We already know what she has to say.*>

<*How's Cheeky?*> Nance asked. <*Is she alive?*>

<*Burned…burned a lot, but I have the med-nano working on her. Thank stars we got the bay upgraded on the* Intrepid.>

<*Nance. Finaeus. What are you up to down there?*> Jessica asked. <*Because whatever it is, it better be good.*>

There was no response, but Jessica did breathe a sigh of relief as she felt the cold air blowing through the vents. Internal readouts listed it as nearly one-hundred percent nitrogen. Cold, but deadly.

She wondered at how she could feel the air so well, and then pain flooded her mind as she realized that her skin had been exposed to vacuum.

<*Damn… I thought this shipsuit was airtight!*>

She dampened the sensation as her body's med-readout showed that capillaries across her entire body had burst when Sabrina vented the atmosphere.

<*Thanks for the warning.*> she said to Iris.

<*I knew you'd survive,*> the AI replied. <*But maybe you should get in a suit now. There's time. We're still five minutes from those TSF ships.*>

Jessica rose on shaky feet to see Trevor standing behind her with an EVA suit.

<*Thanks,*> she said with a mental smile—too exhausted to give a physical one.

<*Sure thing,*> Trevor replied. <*I wouldn't want you dying in your moment of triumph.*>

<*What a rush,*> Jessica said shakily. <*When this is over, I'm gonna fuck your brains out.*>

Trevor barked a laugh that she was able to hear through the thin atmosphere in the ship while he held up the EVA suit for her to climb into.

Once it was on, she realized how cold she'd just been—a far cry from feeling like she was going to burn to death a few minutes earlier.

<*OK, I think we're ready down here,*> Nance said. <*You did get the hackit in their STC, right?*>

<*We did,*> Cargo replied. <*But that was so we could change the gate's destination. We don't have a mirror, so what's the use?*>

<*Well,*> Finaeus said, his voice weak but triumphant. <*What if we did have a mirror?*>

<*Then I'm activating the hackit,*> Iris announced.

<*And I'm boosting for the gate,*> Jessica added.

She calculated their best vector and decided to arc gently toward the floating ring. No point in giving their destination away to the TSF fleet too soon.

<*Krissy's hailing us again,*> Sabrina said.

Jessica debated putting the admiral on, but Finaeus spoke up. <*Please put her on.*>

<*That was some impressive flying,*> Krissy said as Sabrina connected her with their shipnet. <*But there's no feasible way you can escape now—I can't hold my ships back any longer. Come in and I'll do what I can to protect you all.*>

<*Sorry, dear. My Krissy Wrentham,*> Finaeus replied. <*Things aren't going to play out like that—though I really did want to see you once more.*>

<*Finaeus…what do you mean?*> Krissy asked, worry in her voice. <*The gate, what are you doing?*>

<*We're getting out of here, that's what,*> Finaeus replied. <*I…I love you, Krissy. Stay safe.*>

Jessica removed everyone else from the conversation, allowing Krissy and her father to have a few private moments as the ship raced toward the gate.

Most of the TSF ships were well behind them, boosting out from Gisha Station, though a few were near the gate. Jessica held her breath, hoping that they would hold their fire.

A few shots did lance out, but the stasis shield still had enough power to shed their beams, especially now that no one was shooting at them from behind, and the cooling vanes were deployed.

Ahead, the Ford-Svaiter mirrors around the rim of the jump gate began to flare, antimatter reactions generating negative energy that the mirrors directed into a single, roiling point.

<I have confirmation from the hackit. It's aligned the gate with New Canaan. We're good for insertion,> Iris said. *<Or whatever it's called when we go through one of these things.>*

Jessica saw a strange field emanate from the front of the ship, and watched in awe as the mirrors on the gate turned toward them, moving the roiling ball of negative energy until it met with the field in front of *Sabrina*.

Then the ship's sensors went blind and the universe ceased to exist.

A FAREWELL

STELLAR DATE: 07.22.8938 (Adjusted Years)
LOCATION: Sabrina, between Gisha Station and the DSM Ring
REGION: DSM Ring, Grey Wolf System

<Confirm the packet,> Finaeus said. *<You're going to need it.>*

Krissy used the private key her father had given her years ago and unsealed the data packet, confirming its checksums. Her eyes widened as she realized what she was looking at.

Enough dirt on the admiralty to ensure they protected her from the Grey Division.

<How…>

<I always kept one ear to the ground,> Finaeus replied with a mental smile. *<I've used a lot of it over the years, but everything still there is untouched. You'll be able to stay safe—though you may want to examine your position. The Transcend isn't what it used to be. She'll do whatever she can to take you down, Krissy.>*

She took a deep breath. If what was in the data packet was true, her father's crazy theories were real. The Transcend was in great danger—and her father getting to New Canaan would be the first step in saving it. In saving them all.

<You be safe Finaeus…Dad,> Krissy said. *<If you can get all this sorted out, maybe we'll actually get to meet properly soon.>*

<Dad. Been a while since you called me that, Krissy. Sounds nice.>

She winced at the pain she heard in her father's voice. Their prior encounters had often ended with her saying unkind things to him. Not her proudest moments.

<I'm sorry. I love you, Dad.>

<I love you too, dear.>

The connection cut out, and Krissy watched the scan data flow in from where she stood in Gisha Station's auxiliary STC.

The *Sabrina* was racing toward the gate, moving fast after its breakaway around the mining ring. Around her, engineers were frantically trying to understand how the Inner Stars freighter had taken control of the jump gate, while Krissy allowed herself a small smile.

In a way, it was good to know that they hadn't figured everything out. That a crew of pirates, an ancient TBI agent, and an old man, centuries past his prime, could best them.

Maybe it meant that there was hope for what lay ahead. If this little group could stand against the TSF, maybe the colonists at New Canaan could furnish some solution to the looming war—and the poison she now knew lay within the heart of the Transcend.

"How are they doing this?" Stationmaster Lloyd asked from Krissy's side. "It's like they have total control."

"I guess they've a few tricks we've never seen," Krissy replied.

Lloyd cast her a sharp look. "You're surprisingly blasé about this."

Krissy laughed. "I'm alive, my father is alive, Bes is dead. This is an outcome I can live with."

"That's almost treasonous," Lloyd said.

"Almost," Krissy nodded in agreement.

"Something's happening," one of the civilian engineers called out. "The ring's moving!"

Krissy's eyes snapped to the main holotank. Sure enough, a control thruster on the ring was firing, turning it just as *Sabrina*'s mysterious new mirror touched the ball of negative energy on the focal line.

And then the ship was gone.

A wave of panic washed over her. "Was it destroyed? What happened?"

"No…it just changed their destination," the engineer replied. "It' s…"

"What is it?" Krissy snapped.

"Their destination…it's extragalactic."

PERSEUS ARM

STELLAR DATE: 07.22.8938 (Adjusted Years)
LOCATION: Unknown
REGION: Milky Way Galaxy

<*Oh shit!*> Finaeus cried out.

<*What? What's happening? Are we dead?*> Jessica replied.

From what she could see there was nothing outside the ship. Not the same sort of nothing as the dark layer. *That* was still a plane of existence. Here, as far as scan could tell, nothing existed beyond the small bubble of space wrapped around the ship.

<*Pull up the scan logs. Did the ring move right before we hit it?*> Finaeus asked, desperation in his voice.

<*On it,*> Nance said over the shipnet. <*Crap, it did! What does that mean?*>

Finaeus let loose a string of curses that almost made no sense, unless he was naming every deity in some pantheon Jessica had never heard of.

<*I'll tell you what it means. It means we're not going to New Canaan.*>

<*Then where?*> Cargo asked.

<*Fucked if I know,*> Finaeus said.

<*Then shut it off,*> Jessica said. <*Get us out of whatever this thing is and back into normal space.*>

<*Don't you think I'm trying?*> Finaeus shouted back. <*This isn't exactly the normal way to do this, you know! I wasn't even certain it would work. If Nance hadn't had a brilliant idea at the last minute we would have been obliterated.*>

<*Wow…really not feeling better here,*> Trevor said.

<*We could just kill the stasis field,*> Nance suggested. <*The bubble should just collapse and drop us back into normal space.*>

<*And hit a star? Are you crazy?*> Finaeus asked.

<*Better than winding up in some other galaxy—or worse…*>

Jessica didn't want to know what 'or worse' could be, and didn't ask.

<*Do it,*> Cargo ordered.

<*Disabling the stasis field,*> Nance reported.

An instant later, regular space snapped back into place around the ship and Jessica let out a long sigh of relief.

A field of stars never looked so beautiful.

And unrecognizable.

<*Where are we?*> she asked.

<*Triangulating,*> Iris said.

<*Still in the Milky Way,*> Sabrina reported.

<*It's…the Perseus Arm!*> Iris announced.

<*Perseus!*> Several voices yelled at once.

* * * * *

Breathable air had been restored to the ship, and the reactors were running on minimum, slowly charging the SC Batts while the ship cooled down.

The crew—minus Cheeky who was still unconscious, and Piya, who had written herself into static storage and couldn't be re-initialized until Cheeky's brain had recovered—were assembled on the bridge.

"I still can't believe it," Nance said. "Perseus. We have to be at least nine-thousand light-years from New Canaan now."

"Way to go, Finaeus," Trevor chuckled.

Cargo scowled at him. "It's really not that funny."

Trevor shrugged. "I'm just happy to be alive, and not adrift in the intergalactic void. Considering our options over the previous couple of hours were jail, being blown up, disappearing into a black hole, getting blown up again, being smashed into bits by negative energy, or dying a slow death in the deep black, the Perseus Arm is practically a miracle."

A smile crept across Cargo's face and he began to laugh. "Well…when you put it that way."

Jessica began to chuckle, and Finaeus joined in, and then Nance and Trevor. A minute later everyone was still laughing their asses off when Sabrina broke in.

<Seriously? You organics pick now to lose your minds? We have to figure out how to get back!>

"Sorry," Jessica gasped. "We're just all really glad to still be alive, I guess."

<Well, I've picked up noise from a star nearby, so we're not beyond the edges of civilization at least.> Sabrina said.

"Oh really?" Finaeus asked. "Settlements out this far? You realize what that means, right?"

Jessica did. "We're in Orion space and at least twenty years from home."

"Bingo."

"Then we have some time on our hands," Jessica grinned. "Join me in our cabin, would you, Trevor?"

* * * * *

Nance couldn't sleep.

The events of the last day filled her mind, making it feel as though it would burst. Somehow, Erin seemed oblivious to it, off with the other AI, doing whatever it was they did in their little Expanse on *Sabrina*.

But she knew what she did.

There had been no stealth ship at Gisha Station, and no incoming fire from Bes's destroyer. That had been her doing, as had the enlarged opening in the stasis shield that allowed the TSF soldiers to attack, and finally the solution that had helped Finaeus get the Ford-Svaiter mirror to work.

Except it hadn't been her. It had been the thing inside of her, the thing put there by the entity she had met so long ago on Senzee station.

The Caretaker.

THE END

Jessica and the crew of *Sabrina* are a long way from home, on the far edges of human expansion. Now, faced with a twenty-year journey to New Canaan, they must first repair their ship, help Cheeky recover, and figure out the best route home.

A route that starts with a little trip to a place Jessica likes to think of as The World at the Edge of Space.

Pick up The World at the Edge of Space for just $2.99 on Amazon.

If you're looking for another quick read, and haven't checked out Rika Mechanized yet, it's a great start to a new part of the Aeon 14 universe.

THANK YOU

If you've enjoyed reading The Gate at the Grey Wolf Star, a review on Amazon.com and/or goodreads.com would be greatly appreciated.

To get the latest news and access to free novellas and short stories, sign up on the Aeon 14 mailing list: www.aeon14.com/signup.

M. D. Cooper

BOOKS BY M. D. COOPER

Aeon 14

The Intrepid Saga

- Book 1: Outsystem
- Book 2: A Path in the Darkness
- Book 3: Building Victoria
- The Intrepid Saga Omnibus – *Also contains Destiny Lost, book 1 of the Orion War series*
- Destiny Rising – *Special Author's Extended Edition comprised of both Outsystem and A Path in the Darkness with over 100 pages of new content.*

The Orion War

- Book 1: Destiny Lost
- Tales of the Orion War: Set the Galaxy on Fire
- Book 2: New Canaan
- Book 3: Orion Rising
- Tales of the Orion War: Ignite the Stars Within (Fall 2017)
- Tales of the Orion War: Burn the Galaxy to Ash (Fall 2017)
- Book 4: Starfire (coming in 2018)
- Book 5: Return to Sol (coming in 2018)

Visit www.aeon14.com/orionwar to learn what's next in the Orion War.

Perilous Alliance (Expanded Orion War - with Chris J. Pike)

- Book 1: Close Proximity
- Book 2: Strike Vector (August 2017)
- Book 3: Collision Course (October 2017)

Rika's Marauders (Age of the Orion War)

- Prequel: Rika Mechanized

- Book 1: Rika Outcast (August 2017)

Perseus Gate (Age of the Orion War)

- Episode 1: The Gate at the Grey Wolf Star
- Episode 2: The World at the Edge of Space (July 2017)
- Episode 3: A Dance on the Moons of Serenity (August 2017)

The Warlord (Before the Age of the Orion War)

- Book 1: A Woman Without a Country (Sept 2017)

The Sentience Wars: Origins (With James S. Aaron)

- Book 1: Lyssa's Dream (July 2017)
- Book 2: Lyssa's Run (October 2017)

The Sol Dissolution

- The 242 - Venusian Uprising (In The Expanding Universe 2 anthology)

The Delta Team Chronicles (Expanded Orion War)

- A "Simple" Kidnapping (Pew! Pew! Volume 1)
- The Disney World (Pew! Pew! Volume 2 – Sept 2017)

Touching the Stars

Book 1: The Girl Who Touched the Stars

ABOUT THE AUTHOR

Michael Cooper likes to think of himself as a jack of all trades (and hopes to become master of a few). When not writing, he can be found writing software, working in his shop at his latest carpentry project, or likely reading a book.

He shares his home with a precocious young girl, his wonderful wife (who also writes), two cats, a never-ending list of things he would like to build, and ideas...

Find out what's coming next at www.aeon14.com

52569225R00079

Made in the USA
San Bernardino, CA
23 August 2017